WARRIORS

BATTLES of the CLANS

WARRIORS

THE NEW PROPHECY

POWER OF THREE

OMEN OF THE STARS

EXPLORE THE
WARRIORS WORLD

Also by ERIN HUNTER

SEEKERS

WARRIORS

BATTLES of the CLANS

ERIN HUNTER

ILLUSTRATED by WAYNE McLOUGHLIN

HARPER

An Imprint of HarperCollinsPublishers

Battles of the Clans
Text copyright © 2010 by Working Partners Limited
Series created by Working Partners Limited
Illustrations copyright © 2010 by Wayne McLoughlin
Warriors Adventure Game © 2010 by Working Partners Limited
"The Deluge" © 2010 by Working Partners Limited
HarperCollins Children's Books,
a division of HarperCollins Publishers,
10 East 53rd Street, New York, NY 10022.
www.harpercollinschildrens.com

Library of Congress Cataloging-in-Publication Data
Hunter, Erin.
 Battles of the clans / by Erin Hunter ; [illustrations by Wayne McLoughlin] — 1st ed.
 p. cm. — (Warriors)
 Summary: Onestar, leader of WindClan, introduces two young kittypets to the
warrior code, the history of each of the Clans, and legendary battles that have been
fought.
 ISBN 978-0-06-170230-3 (trade bdg.) — ISBN 978-0-06-170231-0 (lib. bdg.)
 [1. Cats—Fiction. 2. Battles—Fiction. 3. Fantasy.] I. McLoughlin, Wayne, ill.
II. Title.
PZ7.H916625Bat 2010   2009053391
[Fic]—dc22   CIP
                                                                          AC

Typography by Hilary Zarycky
10 11 12 13 14 CG/LP/WOR 10 9 8 7 6 5 4 3 2 1
❖
First Edition

For William and Oliver, two splendid boys

Special thanks to Victoria Holmes

CONTENTS

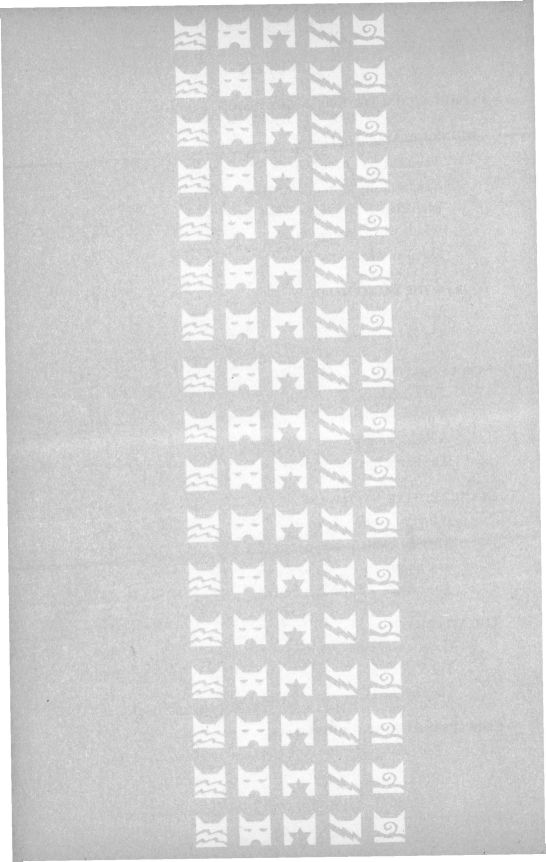

INTRODUCTION:
THE FIRE IN OUR BLOOD

❊

hallo, Ashfoot, who's this? A couple of strays found on the moor? And they asked to see me? Well, bring them into my den; let's have a look at them. You're not Clan cats, are you? I don't recognize your scent—and there's a whiff of kittypet about you, if I'm not mistaken. Don't look so scared. We don't really line our nests with the bones of kittypets. See? Just moss and feathers. Bones are much too uncomfortable to lie on.

I am Onestar, leader of WindClan. And this is the WindClan camp.

You want to know what it's like to be a Clan cat, don't you? About the code that binds us and gives us the courage to survive, about the Gatherings, where we meet in peace for the flicker of a full moon to share tongues and wisdom and news. And the battles—oh, yes, the battles. I can see from the way your eyes gleam that this is what interests you most: the blood-soaked history of the four Clans, the fighting skills passed from mentor to apprentice.

Every young warrior dreams of going into battle. What better way to prove your loyalty to your Clan than to risk your own blood? And what better chance of personal glory? The greatest warriors are remembered by every Clan and are honored in the stars by our ancestors.

But don't go thinking that warrior cats crave only spilled blood, the chill of a rallying yowl, and the heat of endless battles. Our lives are about so much more than fighting. We live to serve our Clan however we can, hunting for fresh-kill, building safe, sheltering dens for the queens and kits, paying our debt to our elders by caring for them before they go to join StarClan. Look around you: No cats are bleeding or limping from battle wounds; fur is flat and smooth, not ruffled in anger; there are no furious yowls carried on the air, just the purr of queens nursing their kits and the rumble of elders telling stories.

What's that? Have I *killed* another cat in battle? What a question! You still have much to learn about the ways of warrior cats. The warrior code says: *An honorable warrior does not need to kill other cats to win his battles.* Victory can be won without spilling blood.

Going into battle is the hardest decision a Clan leader can make. If I send my warriors to fight against another Clan, it hurts me more than any claw or tooth ripping through my pelt. Battle is the very last resort, and I, like all Clan leaders, will do anything to avoid spilling the blood of my warriors or those of another Clan.

Come with me, kittypets; I'll take you to each of the territories and introduce you to these sometime allies, sometime enemies, and you will learn more about the battles of the Clans. Luckily for you, the Clans are at peace right now. There is a Gathering tomorrow night, so many of us will be resting before the late night and the journey to the island.

But remember, we have our claws and our teeth for a reason, and my warriors are as brave and skilled as any here. When the time for talking has passed, battle may be the only option. And never let it be said that WindClan cats are not to be feared when the rallying cry goes up: *Warriors, attack!*

PART ONE:
TECHNIQUES AND
STRATEGIES

THUNDERCLAN

THUNDERCLAN FACTS

Leader: Firestar
Deputy: Brambleclaw
Medicine cat: Jayfeather
Hunting territory: Forest
Camp: Stone hollow
Unique battle skill: Fighting in dense undergrowth

Brambleclaw's Welcome

O nestar? Is something wrong? Who are your companions? Ah, a pair of curious kittypets. Welcome to ThunderClan. Our camp is on the other side of that row of thornbushes, sheltered by the cliffs of stone. Forgive me if I don't invite you in. I have only your word and Onestar's that you haven't come to learn more than we are willing to share.

You want to know about ThunderClan's battle tactics? Well,

look around. Notice the brambles and ferns crowding in on you, blocking your sight. We see them as opportunities for camouflage and causing confusion to the enemy when we pounce on them from every side. We have been trained to fight in these enclosed spaces, paw-to-paw, with nowhere for the trespassers to flee. We can spin on the tip of a tail, find strength in a strike where there is barely room to draw back our paws, leap from a standstill while our enemy is struggling to turn around.

Firestar has even started holding training sessions in the trees so we can leap from branch to branch like squirrels and drop onto our enemies' heads while they're still trying to find our trail on the ground.

The forest is a magnificent place to fight. This is where we hone our stalking skills, our ability to creep up on our prey unnoticed and pounce with one brutal, effective leap.

You want to know the *best* ThunderClan battle tactic? *Best?* Well, without giving away too much, let me just say that every ThunderClan apprentice loves to learn the Lightning Strike. Just like a bolt of lightning, it is straightforward, swift, and deadly. It's fitting that ThunderClan should be able to summon up a storm, don't you think?

Special Battle Tactic:
Bumblepaw Learns the Lightning Strike

"ey! You guys! Wait till you hear what we did in training today!" Bumblepaw burst through the thorns and raced across the sunbaked earth to the elderflower bush where ThunderClan's elders slept. Two apprentices, Dovepaw and Ivypaw, were lying outside with Lionblaze and Purdy. The remains of a mouse and a thrush lay beside them, still warm and tempting, but Bumblepaw was too full of his news to leave room for any appetite.

"Are you going to tell us, or are we supposed to guess?" demanded Ivypaw.

Bumblepaw blinked. "Mousewhisker and Thornclaw taught us the best thing ever! It's a kind of attack called a Lightning Strike, and it's amazing! There's no way we could lose a battle with this!"

Lionblaze snorted. "It takes more than one tactic to win a battle," he warned. "But you're right: The Lightning Strike is good for chasing out trespassers because it's fast and takes the enemy by surprise."

"Just like lightning!" Bumblepaw agreed. He noticed that Dovepaw and Ivypaw were looking blank. "It's like this," he explained. "You two sit over there"—he gave them a nudge with his nose until they shuffled away from Lionblaze and Purdy—"and pretend you're invading my territory."

"Are we enemies, too?" asked Purdy, sounding amused.

"No, you're trees that I'm going to hide behind. First I'm going to track the enemy patrol through the forest."

Dovepaw and Ivypaw watched wide-eyed as Bumblepaw crouched down behind the other cats and started to creep forward with his belly fur brushing the ground.

"You look like you're stalking prey!" Dovepaw gasped.

Bumblepaw popped his head above Purdy's back. "That's exactly what I'm doing. And *you* are my prey!" He ducked down again and took another step. "You should have seen Thornclaw showing us this move this morning. He was lower than a snake's belly! No cat would have seen him coming."

"You should watch Sandstorm sometime, too," Lionblaze put in. "She can track a mouse from the other side of the forest."

Bumblepaw frowned at him. "Trees don't talk!" he reminded the warrior. "This is my demonstration."

Lionblaze flicked his tail against Bumblepaw's shoulder. "Sorry!" he whispered.

Bumblepaw reached Purdy's nose and stretched his neck until he could see Dovepaw and Ivypaw. Still crouching, he explained, "Once the enemy has been spotted, we sneak up until we can almost touch them. Then we wait for the patrol leader's command—which will be a silent tail signal, obviously—and *pounce!*" He pushed down with his hind paws and sprang out from behind Purdy. He landed on Dovepaw's haunches, careful to keep his claws sheathed, and knocked her gently aside. Then he spun around and reared up toward Ivypaw, striking the air with his front paws.

"Got you!" he yowled.

Ivypaw twitched one ear. "You're hardly the scariest warrior in the forest. You didn't even touch me!"

"I wouldn't keep my claws hidden if it were a real battle, mouse-brain!" Bumblepaw pointed out as he dropped back onto all fours. "I'd bite you and scratch you and slash you with my hind claws until you begged for mercy!"

Lionblaze interrupted him as Dovepaw's and Ivypaw's eyes grew even wider. "This tree is breaking its vow of silence to remind you not to give the new apprentices nightmares," he warned.

Bumblepaw let his fur lie back down. "Well, you get the idea. We strike hard and fast, pouncing all at once to cause as much confusion as we can. Mousewhisker said to scratch the enemies' ears because they will bleed more than anywhere else, and make it look as if the invaders are hurt more than they really are. Cunning, huh?"

He gazed triumphantly at the other apprentices. Dovepaw still looked startled, but Ivypaw didn't seem so impressed. "That's not a battle tactic," she complained. "That's just attacking the enemy."

"Wait, you haven't heard the rest of the move," Bumblepaw told her. "This is the really clever bit. After our first attack, our patrol leader gives the order to retreat into the trees. The enemy thinks we've given up! But we don't run far. We stay quiet and watchful, waiting until the invading cats relax, assuming that we've disappeared into the forest to lick our wounds. They won't expect us to attack them again so soon, not here. After all, lightning doesn't strike twice in the same place, does it?" He looked at his audience. "Does it?" he prompted them.

"Er, no, it doesn't," Dovepaw agreed.

"But it does this time!" Bumblepaw declared. "As soon as the enemy drops their guard, we strike again, as hard and fast as before, same formation, same attacking moves. Ha! That's the last thing those mangy crow-furs were expecting!" He leaped forward with his front paws outstretched, imagining his opponents flinching away from him.

"Strike twice in the same place and our enemies will flee in panic, knowing we have the strength to attack anywhere, anytime. ThunderClan will become known as *LightningClan!*"

FOREST ATTACK: HOW THUNDERCLAN KEEPS THE ELEMENT OF SURPRISE

1. Move quietly and communicate with signals. Cracking twigs, startled birds, and rustling bracken will tell the enemy exactly where you are.

2. Keep downwind of the trespassers so that your scent doesn't give you away.

3. Look for freshly broken twigs, overturned leaves on the forest floor, remains of prey, or a clump of fur caught on a bramble. Any animal that moves through the forest leaves behind signs that it's passed by—and signs like this could lead you straight to the invaders.

4. Keep your mouth open to search for unfamiliar scents. Be careful: If there is scent when there is no breeze to carry it through the forest, it could mean that your enemy is very close by.

5. Light-colored pelts are easily seen against brown and green foliage, so stay in the thickest cover. Keep low—the enemy will be looking for movement at normal head height, not close to the ground.

6. Never miss an opportunity to perfect your tracking ability. In the nursery, kits sneak up on their mothers and pounce with their moss-soft paws. Apprentices leap out on one another from behind bushes and tree stumps. These are more than just games. One day, these skills could save your life and defend your Clan.

Dustpaw Speaks: Shadows in the Forest

I hurled myself up the tree trunk with my front claws stretched out and my ears flattened. Above me, the fluffy gray tail whisked sideways along a narrow branch and vanished. The faintest rustle of leaves told me that the squirrel had leaped to safety in the neighboring tree.

"Fox dung!" I hissed under my breath, hoping I could catch it before Tigerclaw noticed I'd been too slow up the trunk.

I scrambled onto the branch to follow the squirrel, but it swayed beneath me, spilling me out of the tree. *Help!* With a yowl, I thrashed my front paws until my claws sank into the bark above my head. Hot-furred with embarrassment, I clung on with my hind legs dangling beneath me, trying to catch my breath.

"Tell me, Dustpaw," came a politely interested voice below, "when Redtail taught you to swing on branches, did he ever mention that climbing skills could be used to catch prey as well?"

Gritting my teeth, I hauled myself back onto the branch. I knew it wasn't worth trying to defend myself; Tigerclaw would only take the opportunity to have another dig at my mentor, who was back in the camp with a bellyache after eating an old blackbird. A rustle of leaves on the far side of the tree made me stiffen. Was it another squirrel? Great StarClan, did every squirrel in the forest live in this tree?

I peered past the trunk, trying to see a fluffy gray shape among the leaves. There was a soft *chack*, followed by the sound of tiny paws pattering along a branch. Suddenly a twig cracked behind me, and I realized that it was the same squirrel taunting me by running circles around my branch. *Just you wait till I see you on the ground, you mangy piece of fresh-kill.*

Scowling, I lowered myself backward down the trunk and jumped onto the ground. Tigerclaw was waiting for me at the foot of the tree, his hefty paws planted squarely on the leaf mold.

Darkstripe and Longtail stood behind him, watching me with scorn in their eyes. For a moment, I was tempted to challenge them to catch a squirrel from the trees—every cat knew that only the fastest and most experienced hunters went after squirrels above the ground. But I figured that Tigerclaw would know too many ways to punish a cheeky apprentice, so I kept quiet.

A skinny black cat padded up to me. "Bad luck," Ravenpaw mewed. His green eyes were sympathetic. "I wouldn't be brave enough to climb that high!"

Tigerclaw glanced sideways at his apprentice, and I winced at the contempt in his gaze. "Which is why I sent Dustpaw after that squirrel. I'd be amazed if you managed to catch whitecough," the warrior growled. He lifted his head, and a shaft of early morning sun slicing through the trees dappled his fur with frosted gold. "Come on, let's get back to camp," he ordered. He led the way along a narrow track through the ferns. Longtail and Darkstripe crowded after him—*that's right, stick close to Tigerclaw if you think it makes you better warriors.* Ravenpaw fell into line behind them, his tail so low that the tip left a tiny furrow in the bits of dried leaves.

I looked up at the trees, wondering where the squirrel had gone. If it had a nest close by, it would be worth coming back to this place to catch it on the ground, foraging. Just then, I heard a faint noise, like a twig snapping, and whirled around. A flash of dark fur closely followed by a splash of white; the outline of pricked ears; what looked like the tip of a tail flickering above the ferns.

"Have you grown roots, Dustpaw? Bluestar is expecting us back this side of moonhigh, you know." Tigerclaw was watching me from the end of the path, his tail twitching impatiently.

"I think we're being invaded!" I hissed, angling my ears toward the place where I'd seen the passing shapes.

Tigerclaw followed my gaze, stiffening when he saw the line of cats padding stealthily between the slender gray tree trunks.

"ShadowClan!" he snarled. The fur along his spine bristled. "Patrol! Come here!" he called softly. The ferns trembled as Ravenpaw, Longtail, and Darkstripe trotted back to us. They stared through the trees in horror at the ShadowClan warriors heading for the center of ThunderClan's territory.

"Those mangy crow-food eaters!" growled Darkstripe, unsheathing his claws.

Longtail bunched his hindquarters underneath him. "Should I go and get help?" he offered.

Tigerclaw shook his head. "There's no time. We must try to head them off ourselves."

Darkstripe gulped. "But there are only five of us. It looks like they've brought the whole Clan to invade!"

"They'll rip us to shreds!" Ravenpaw whimpered.

"Not if we rip them first," Tigerclaw vowed. "We'll use the Lightning Strike: Hit them hard and fast, retreat, then attack again from the same direction."

Squirrels, I thought. *Squirrels running in circles.*

"Squirrels!" I said out loud.

Tigerclaw looked at me as if I'd gone mad. "No, ShadowClan invaders," he growled. "Great StarClan, if you can't catch a single piece of prey, how am I supposed to lead you into battle?"

"No, we have to think like squirrels," I insisted. "At least, the squirrel that I lost up that tree. He circled me, making me think there were two of him. It . . . it was confusing."

Darkstripe snorted. "Okay, you go back and persuade your fluffy-tailed friend to help us, and we'll take care of the fighting," he suggested with a meaningful look at Tigerclaw.

But the dark tabby warrior was staring thoughtfully at me. "Go on," he prompted.

My fur felt hot and prickly. "I . . . I haven't exactly thought it out," I stammered, "but I thought if we did a Lightning Strike on one side, then regrouped on the other side and . . . er . . . pretended to be different cats, ShadowClan might think there were more of us. It would be like a . . . a double Lightning Strike."

"Oh, yes, because ShadowClan warriors are blind and have no sense of smell, so they think every ThunderClan cat looks like us," sneered Longtail. He flicked his tail.

Tigerclaw raised one front paw. "Wait. This might work." He turned to face the other cats. "If we attack fast enough and cause enough confusion, the invaders won't have a chance to recognize us. You three, follow my orders, and don't lose sight of the rest of the patrol."

Whoa! Tigerclaw was actually going to listen to my idea?

"Ravenpaw, go to the ravine and tell Bluestar what is happening," he ordered. "If the plan doesn't work, we'll need backup fast."

Ravenpaw vanished into the ferns like a snake.

Tigerclaw spun around and leaped through the trees in the direction of the invaders. Longtail and Darkstripe sprang after him, and I followed. *My first real battle!* The blood roared in my ears, and I opened my mouth wide to inhale the scents of the strangers that tainted the fresh, green-tasting air.

"Keep still!" Tigerclaw hissed over his shoulder. "Enemy dead ahead."

I peered over the heads of the other cats to see the line of ShadowClan warriors slinking along a fox path. They were moving slower now, as if they were unsure exactly where the ThunderClan camp was.

"Ready?" Tigerclaw demanded. *"Attack!"*

Without checking to see if we were following, he plunged out of the undergrowth and leaped with a roar onto the cat at the back of the ShadowClan line. The short-tailed brown tom didn't have time to let out a yowl before he was knocked to the ground. Tigerclaw used the tom's face to push off with his hind paws as he launched himself toward the next cat. Darkstripe tore past and sank his outstretched front claws into another warrior, while Longtail and I tackled the brown tom at the back as he tried to struggle to his feet.

The cats at the head of the line came racing back, teeth bared and hackles raised. There was no time to think about battle moves, about balancing my weight evenly on my hind paws and landing each blow perfectly. Instead, I spun and slashed and snarled until the trees blurred around me. Delicate ear skin caught under one of my claws; with a wrench, I ripped my paw clear and felt a thin spray of blood land on my muzzle.

"ThunderClan, retreat!" Tigerclaw's command cut through the pant and hiss of the fighting. I sheathed my claws and sprang into the nearest patch of ferns. Glancing back, I saw Longtail blink in satisfaction and raise one front paw to check his claws for trapped fur. Out in the open, the invaders began to talk.

"Did we beat them?" That was the short-tailed tom, who was bleeding heavily from one ear.

The white cat with black paws who had led the patrol looked around. I realized that it was Blackfoot, the ShadowClan deputy; I'd seen him and a couple of the other cats at a Gathering.

"We must have," Blackfoot growled. "Mouse-hearted cowards. They can't even defend their own territory!"

"Should we keep going?" asked a red-furred she-cat. Her eyes gleamed, and she seemed the least daunted by the attack out of all of them.

"In a moment, Russetfur," said Blackfoot. "We'll let Stumpytail get his breath back first."

"This way," Tigerclaw whispered. Turning with difficulty in the crowded space, he pushed his way out of the ferns on the other side from the fox path. He drew the tip of his tail across his mouth, warning us to keep silent, then padded softly in a circle around the ShadowClan warriors, leaping across the fox path when they were out of sight and plunging into the undergrowth on the far side. There were more brambles than ferns here, and I bit my tongue to stop myself from yelping when thorns scratched my spine.

"Quick!" Tigerclaw hissed. "Before they start moving again." He forced his way through the tangled prickles until we had drawn level with the invaders. "Remember to scuff up the sand with your paws so that they can't see us clearly. Now!"

He hurled himself out of the branches with Darkstripe at his heels. Longtail followed, and I pushed out after them. My head was still ringing from the last skirmish, and my legs felt trembly from the race around to the other side of the path. But the plan seemed to have worked: The ShadowClan warriors reacted as if this were a completely new patrol come to attack them.

"Where did the others go?" panted Stumpytail, ducking out of the way of Longtail's flailing front paws.

"Keep an eye behind you," warned Blackfoot through clenched teeth. "In case they try to sneak up on us."

"I'm sure I heard one of them call another one Longtail," hissed Russetfur. "I'll remember that name."

I blinked. *Are you sure about that, Russetfur?* "Hey, Runningwind!" I yowled. "I need some help over here!"

Longtail looked at me in surprise. He started to say something, then nodded. "Coming, Graypaw!" He sprang over Stumpytail, who had been rolled over by Darkstripe, and kept pace with me as we trapped a pale tabby tom against the brambles and pulled out a few clawfuls of silvery fur.

"Good strike, Lionheart!" Darkstripe called behind us, as Tigerclaw sent Blackfoot stumbling against a rock.

The massive dark tabby spun around to face his warriors. "ThunderClan, away!"

Dodging a swipe from Russetfur, who had come to rescue the silver tabby, I leaped sideways into the brambles. Tigerclaw and the others joined me, their flanks heaving. Kicked-up sand and dust clung to the blood that had splashed on their fur, and one of Darkstripe's eyes was half-closed from a well-placed blow.

"Final strike," hissed Tigerclaw. "Longtail and Darkstripe, you stay here. Dustpaw, come with me. When I give the signal, attack from both sides and make it seem as if the whole of ThunderClan is behind us. Okay?"

Grim nods; then Tigerclaw plunged back into the brambles, leaving me scrambling to catch up. We crossed the path out of sight from the ShadowClan warriors and returned to our original strike point. The invading cats were huddled in the dirt, staring around as they waited for the next attack.

"Do you think we should leave before they come back?" Stumpytail whispered.

Tigerclaw didn't give the other invaders a chance to reply. "Attack!" he screeched, flinging himself through the ferns. From the far side of the path came the sound of Darkstripe and Longtail crashing out of the brambles, blood-spattered hackles raised and claws unsheathed.

"Over here, Redtail!" I yowled over my shoulder as I leaped into the fray.

"We've trapped them, Bluestar!" Longtail added.

The ShadowClan cats whirled in alarm. "They've brought the whole Clan!" gasped Russetfur.

Blackfoot paused, muzzle-to-muzzle with Tigerclaw. "You win this time," he snarled. "But watch your borders, because we'll be back!" Then he lifted his head and called, "ShadowClan, retreat!"

Tigerclaw stepped back, giving a flick of his tail to warn the

ThunderClan cats to do the same. I watched in satisfaction as the ShadowClan cats limped past, leaving a trail of scarlet dots in the sand.

My plan had worked, and my Clan was safe from the ShadowClan invasion.

"THE NIGHT AMBUSH"

shadowclan

Rowanclaw's Welcome

Greetings, Onestar. Why have you come to ShadowClan's territory? Ah, I see you have brought companions. Is WindClan recruiting kittypets now?

Do you really expect me to invite you into our camp and explain why ShadowClan has the most feared warriors in all the

Clans? Our strengths are our secrets, my friend. Would I ask you to train my Clanmates to run as swiftly as you do, or to hunt rabbits? I think not.

But I would not be betraying my role as Blackstar's deputy if I reminded you that ShadowClan earned its name for a reason.

We are night hunters, our senses most alert in the darkness and silence that befuddles other cats. We can slip noiselessly through shadows like fish through black water, and speak to one another without words. Unlike the other Clans, who cling to moonlight or the watchful shine of StarClan, we like the freedom that is found in the darkest nights.

When it comes to battle, we waste no time rallying our warriors with speeches or promises of glory; they know what is expected of them, and they will deliver or face the shame of betraying their

Clan. While the other Clans arrange themselves in lines and circles and elaborate battle plans, we swoop and strike and vanish into the night. We fight to win, nothing else.

Go now, and leave us to train in the dead of night. May StarClan—not ShadowClan—walk in your dreams.

Special Battle Tactic: Tigerheart Teaches the Night Ambush

Gather around, apprentices. I know it's dark, but you can hear my voice, can't you? That's right, over here. No, Olivepaw, you're not going to fall into any foxholes. I checked earlier today that this would be a good place for our ambush practice. Maybe one day you will have to navigate somewhere with holes waiting to trip you up, but hopefully you'll be more experienced by then, and more confident about moving around at night. That's if you live that long, *Scorchpaw.* Come down from that tree *at once.* No, I can't see any better than you can, but I have ears, and a deaf badger would have heard your claws scraping on the bark when you climbed up. And the fact that your scent is now coming from above my head is also a giveaway.

Shrewpaw, Redpaw, Owlpaw, are you here? Good. Now, I want everyone to stand very still and close their eyes. *Who is snoring?* Scorchpaw, that's not nearly as funny as you think it is. Only horses sleep standing up, and if you'd like to go live with them and eat grass all day, I'm sure Blackstar can arrange it.

Right, keep your eyes closed until I tell you. Mouths closed, too, Owlpaw. If I can hear you whispering, then so can the enemy. Use your other senses: What can you hear? Smell? Taste? Feel on your fur? Well? Anyone?

Okay, you can open your mouth if I've asked you a direct question. Good, Shrewpaw. There's a breeze coming from the lake, bringing the scent of water and fish and RiverClan. But not strong enough to suggest they're any closer than their territory. You think you can hear ThunderClan snoring, Scorchpaw? No, you can't. The day Blackstar receives a prophecy about a cat with the ability to hear farther than any other creature, then I'll believe you.

Yes, Redpaw, there is a pair of owls calling to each other beyond the inland border. And one of those kittypets in the Twoleg nest is making its usual fuss about being shut in on a fine night for hunting. So our senses have told us that our territory is empty save for the creatures that live alongside us—no trespassers, nothing that seems out of place. Now, open your eyes. Yes, Olivepaw, it's still very dark. But you can see a little more clearly, can't you? Your eyes have started to adjust to seeing without light. Look at how the trees are outlined against the sky. Down on the ground, you still won't be able to see much, but thicker shadows could be a bush, or even another cat. The more you practice moving around at night, the easier it will become. The other Clans are frightened and baffled by the dark; without the sense of sight, they are as helpless as kits. Only ShadowClan understands the power of the night, and sees it as a strength.

Tonight, we are the ambush patrol. We are going to lie in wait for our enemy, and launch a surprise attack using the darkness to hide us and weaken our rivals before we unsheathe a single claw. First we need to find an attack zone, a place where we can wait without being seen or scented, with enough room to fight when the other cats arrive. Any ideas? Good, Shrewpaw. This gully is just what we're looking for. The sides are high and steep, so if we attack from each end, the enemy won't be able to escape. It's an obvious route to the camp, so we can be confident that any invaders would pass through it. And we can hide in the bushes at the top, with the advantage of attacking from above.

Redpaw, why don't you pick a bush on the side of the gully where we can hide? Hmmm, maybe not so far from the edge. We need to be able to hear our enemy approaching, and see them when they enter the gully. This one's better. Right, squash in, everybody.

So, we're hidden up here, but it would be good to know when the enemy is coming near. We need an early warning patrol, just two cats to keep track of the invaders as they head toward the gully. Imagine that you're following them, and need to warn the ambush patrol to be ready for the attack. What call would you give?

Well, Owlpaw, that was a very good imitation of an owl, but perhaps the patrol might think it was a real owl? What noise would travel clearly on a night like this, but stand out only to cats who live in this part of the territory? How about, *Sssssssss*? Not a snake, Olivepaw. The wind in the trees! Why would that work tonight? That's right, because the breeze coming off the lake shouldn't be enough to move the branches of pine trees. Cats from the other territories won't know that, as this is the only place where pine trees grow by the lake.

What little breeze there is would work in our favor tonight, carrying the scent of the invaders toward us and hiding our own from them. We need to spread out along the top of the gully; if this were a real ambush patrol, we'd have enough cats to line the other side, too. We take up our positions, always within earshot of the leader of the patrol, and wait. Let me see you all waiting now.

What problem would we have if there were moonlight or starlight? That's right, Redpaw. Our shadows. We'd need to stay on the dark side of the bush to keep our outlines hidden, too. Remember, if you can see the enemy, the enemy can see you.

That's why darkness is our ally.

Imagine that the enemy is entering the gully. Who should attack first? Yes, Shrewpaw. The cats at each end of the gully go down first, to trap the enemy and let them know that they are surrounded. Then the others attack, straight down the sides, using the weight of our fall as part of the first blow. Apprentices, strike!

Oof! Redpaw, get your tail out of my mouth! Who's that underneath me? Get up, Olivepaw. No, your tail isn't broken. It's just a bit . . . dented. In a real ambush, no one would get squashed, apart from the enemy. Remember I told you that we'd be in a line along the top of the gully? Well, we'd hold that line as we attacked. What's the use in landing on one or two invading cats in one big lump, leaving their Clanmates free to fight? We'd hope to outnumber them in order to overpower them as swiftly as possible. Once the command to attack has been given, there will be no other orders. You each know what you have to do.

As soon as the enemy surrenders or begs to flee, the fighting stops. Stand still with your head held high. You are a ShadowClan cat; we do not gloat over our defeated enemies. We simply wait for them to leave, knowing they will be in no haste to return. And when they have gone, head for the closest shadow before you go back to the camp. Make no sound. Melt back into the night, so that if our enemy looks back, they see nothing but emptiness. The forest is ours—and we are unseen. The night, the darkness, the cold still air, all belong to ShadowClan. That is our ancestors' gift to us, and we honor their memory with every ambush. It is up to you to prove that you are worthy of that gift and will preserve the night as our greatest weapon.

TAIL SIGNALS

ShadowClan was the first to devise a system of tail signals, which are now used by all four Clans. Generally, the leader of a patrol is responsible for giving the signals; warriors learn to keep the leader's tail in sight at all times and react at once when an order is given.

TAIL HELD ERECT: "Stop."

TAIL RIPPLING: "Move forward with care."

TAIL HELD ERECT AND SWEEPING SLOWLY FROM SIDE TO SIDE: "Retreat silently."

TAIL POINTING LOW, PARALLEL TO GROUND, AND SWEEPING: "Spread out."

TAIL FLATTENED: "Get down."

TAIL BOBBING: "Enemy sighted."

TAIL HOOKED: "Danger."

TAIL POINTED SHARPLY: "Go that way."

TAIL HELD ERECT AND WAVING FROM SIDE TO SIDE: "Stay behind me."

TAIL KINKED OVER BACK: "Follow me."

Blackstar Speaks: Ambush by the Lake

Oakfur, Cedarheart, wait!" I hissed to the warriors ahead of me. My Clanmates stopped on the edge of the hard black stone where Twolegs left their monsters. This was the border of ShadowClan's territory; from here on, we would be in RiverClan. Rowanclaw and Tawnypelt joined us, their eyes glowing in the pale starlight. Clouds covered the moon, a clear advantage to the keenly night-sighted ShadowClan cats. Those mangy RiverClan fish-eaters were about to be taught that promises had to be kept— especially when they were made to ShadowClan. They'd had a chance to solve this peacefully and turned it down.

"Careful!"

"Look, there's one over there!"

"Don't fall in!"

I flattened my ears at the sound of chatter and splashing coming from the end of the halfbridge. The noise traveled clearly over the still water, piercing the pine-scented air in ShadowClan's territory and sending the night prey farther into their holes. There'd be no fresh-kill in my camp tomorrow morning, once again. My Clan would go hungry—and it was RiverClan's fault.

I nodded to Oakfur and Cedarheart, then pointed the tip of my tail toward the small wooden Twoleg nest at the edge of the water. Oakfur and Cedarheart padded across the hard stone and slipped into the shadows around the wooden nest. With my tail straight up in the air, I gestured for Tawnypelt and Rowanclaw to stay behind me. Then I backed under the cover of some ferns growing at the edge of the stone and sat down to wait.

At the last half-moon, I had visited Leopardstar and asked that she stop her patrols from hunting off the halfbridge, which was right at the edge of my Clan's border. RiverClan had been fishing during daylight up till then, attracting the attention of the Twolegs that had made their temporary nests in the clearing on the far side of ShadowClan's territory. Dogs and young Twolegs had come crashing through the pine trees to watch the swimming cats. Their clumsy noise scared off the RiverClan fishers long before the Twolegs arrived, but my Clanmates were left crouching in the scant undergrowth, forced into cover by the intruders and fearing discovery by one of their slavering dogs.

I could have solved the problem with force, extending ShadowClan's territory to include the halfbridge and the place where Twolegs came to launch the creatures that floated on the lake with huge white wings. That would have kept the RiverClan hunting patrols out of the water closest to ShadowClan's territory. But the Clans had been living at the lake for only three moons; I wasn't going to challenge the newly laid-out borders yet, not when the memory of the Great Journey was fresh in every cat's mind. The four Clans had found the lake together, working as allies for the first time that any cat knew, even the elders. However much I wanted to defend this new territory, I didn't want to be the one to break the truce that had saved us when our forest homes were destroyed.

So I had surrendered to a RiverClan border patrol and asked to be taken in peace to Leopardstar. When I told her about the unwanted intrusion by Twolegs coming to investigate the cats fishing off the halfbridge, Leopardstar had sympathized and agreed that things would be different from now on. It seemed as if the bonds forged during the Great Journey had survived the separation into four distinct Clans.

After my visit to Leopardstar, things had indeed been different: Instead of hunting off the halfbridge during the daytime, summoning Twolegs and dogs through the pine trees, RiverClan now fished at night, the time when ShadowClan hunting patrols ventured out. Leopardstar must have known that hunting from the halfbridge at night would only create new problems. If RiverClan was determined to prove that it owed nothing from the Great Journey to the other Clans, then ShadowClan was ready to show the same absence of respect.

A slender gray shape appeared at the edge of the black stone: Mistyfoot, the RiverClan deputy. Stonestream's shadow loomed behind her, followed by the smaller dark brown outline of Voletooth with plump, lazy Swallowtail beside him, given away by her distinctive rolling gait. I narrowed my eyes in satisfaction. One cat each.

"ShadowClan, attack!" I yowled, springing out of the ferns. Halfway across the black stone, Mistyfoot froze. The other RiverClan cats stumbled into her, dropping their fish.

The stone felt rough and hot under my paws as I raced to tackle the RiverClan deputy. I was too fast for Mistyfoot to react; crashing into her, I swept her paws from under her belly and raked my claws along her flank. Beside me, Tawnypelt challenged Swallowtail with a furious hiss; quick as lightning, the RiverClan she-cat spun around and lashed out with her front paws, catching Tawnypelt's ears. Just before I sprang at her, I had time to be impressed that the overfed she-cat could move so neatly. I landed on Swallowtail's back with my claws out; the dark tabby screeched and collapsed to the ground underneath me. I jumped clear as she flopped sideways, trying to crush me. The weight of her body as well as all that fish-tasting fur would have squashed the breath out of me.

A flash of gray at the edge of my sight warned that Stonestream was coming to help his Clanmate; he was met by Oakfur and Tawnypelt, side by side on their hind legs, driving him back with perfectly matched blows. On the far side of the patrol, Rowanclaw had wrestled Voletooth onto his back and was holding his scruff in his jaws while raking the brown tom's belly with his hind legs.

. Behind me, I heard Mistyfoot scramble to her paws. Her breath came in jagged gasps as she snarled, "Blackstar! What are you doing?"

I took a step backward from Swallowtail and flicked my tail from side to side, ordering my Clanmates to surround the hunting patrol and hold them in place. Instantly, my warriors stopped fighting and ran into position. Cedarheart placed himself between Swallowtail and the halfbridge, blocking off that means of escape in case the cats tried to swim away. Rowanclaw and Tawnypelt stood on the far side of the patrol with their backs to the rest of RiverClan's territory. They were vulnerable to being attacked from behind, but the rest of us would keep half an eye on the dense undergrowth, checking for RiverClan warriors coming to their Clanmates' rescue.

Oakfur lined up beside me and curled his lip when Stonestream took a pace toward him. The RiverClan cat blinked and stepped back.

"Wise move," Oakfur growled.

I flashed a glance at him. This was an ambush, not a war. We had won the first skirmish without trouble; from now on, I would handle the talking.

Mistyfoot spoke first. "What in the name of StarClan is going on?" she demanded.

I took a deep breath, letting my anger root me to the ground through my unsheathed claws. Losing my temper would be a sign of weakness, and right now, with my warriors surrounding the RiverClan patrol, I was in control. "Leopardstar promised that you would no longer fish from the halfbridge."

Mistyfoot's eyes flashed. "She promised we would not hunt when Twolegs could see us. We have kept her word."

"You know full well that you are making enough noise to summon Twolegs from the other side of the mountains." My words hissed through my clenched teeth. "How are we supposed to hunt if all our prey has been scared off before our patrols can set out?"

"Perhaps your patrols should learn to hunt better," sneered Voletooth. "Or do you teach your apprentices to sit with their mouths open until a piece of fresh-kill hops inside?"

I ignored Voletooth and spoke to Mistyfoot again. "Every Clan deserves a fair chance to make their new territory their home. Your selfishness is making that harder for us."

"Selfishness?" Mistyfoot echoed. "Since when was feeding our Clanmates selfish? Voletooth is right; you need to stop blaming us for the fact that you can't catch enough prey."

Curling his lip in anger, Rowanclaw swiped the air with his front paw. "We caught you easily enough tonight," he reminded her.

Stonestream leaped forward. "Let's see how brave you are in an honest fight," he challenged. "Instead of sneaking around like foxes!"

Rowanclaw reared up on his hind legs and let the moonlight gleam on his thorn-sharp claws. "Oh, that would be my pleasure," he growled. "Would you like to land the first strike, or shall I?"

"Stop!" yowled Mistyfoot. "This is not a battle we want to fight."

I rounded on her and snarled, "It is a battle that we *will* fight if you don't stop fishing from the halfbridge." But I signaled with my tail for my warriors to leave the RiverClan cats alone.

"You should be ashamed of going back on your leader's promise," I growled to Mistyfoot. "Leopardstar knew what she was agreeing to when I told her the problems you were causing by fishing from the halfbridge. I gave her a fair chance to end it, and she chose not to take it."

Mistyfoot's eyes flashed in the silvery light. "She *chose* to let her hunting patrols do what they do best, and feed their Clanmates."

"Then we'll respond with what we do best, which is fighting without mercy to protect our Clanmates," I replied calmly.

There was a flicker of uncertainty in Mistyfoot's gaze. She knew as well as I did that her warriors stood no chance against mine in a full-scale battle. "Okay, you've made your point," she meowed. "We'll stop fishing from here, and leave you to figure out how to catch the prey in your new territory."

I felt Tawnypelt bristle at the RiverClan deputy's thinly hidden insult. *Don't worry; she's not going to get away with that.* "You think that's it, do you?" I queried. "One halfhearted skirmish and I'll leave you in peace?"

Mistyfoot glanced warily at my patrol. "What else do you want?"

"Fresh-kill," I answered. "You owe us for lost nights of hunting."

Stonestream snorted. "Are you serious? You think we're going to surrender our Clanmates' food to you just because you can skulk in shadows and jump out on cats in their own territory?"

I shook my head. "No. You're going to give us your food because next time we'll do more than skulk in the shadows. Next time we'll bring a patrol right into your camp and rip the ears of each of your warriors so that every Clan knows that Leopardstar cannot keep a promise." I let my claws scrape on the stone, twisting my paws so that the starlight caught the sharpened tips.

Mistyfoot stood rock-still, with only a blink to suggest that she was shocked by my threat. "I . . . I think Leopardstar will agree to what you want," she meowed. "As you say, each Clan should have a time of peace to settle into its new home."

"We'll take half of whatever you catch," I ordered. The knowledge that we had won made my pelt tingle, but I kept my voice steady. "Leave it on the halfbridge at dusk each day until the next half-moon. And if we see a single cat fishing here, we'll be in your camp before you hear us coming."

Mistyfoot dipped her head. "Since we have . . . *removed* the problem, there is no need to mention it at the Gathering, I presume?" She sounded as if she were speaking through gritted teeth. "It is of no interest to the other Clans, after all."

I did my best to hide a flash of amusement. How satisfying to have the RiverClan deputy beg to keep Leopardstar's betrayal a secret from the other Clans. I was half tempted to refuse and let WindClan and ThunderClan know of RiverClan's mean spirit toward their newly settled neighbor. But that would only cause more trouble, and Mistyfoot was right: Peace was needed while our territories were still only half-known.

"Very well," I meowed. The RiverClan deputy turned to leave, but I called her back. I needed to make sure that she knew ShadowClan had not been softened by the Great Journey, that we owed nothing to any Clan and would not shy away from waging war against our former allies.

"Oh, and Mistyfoot? Never trust the shadows. My warriors wear the night like second pelts. If you wrong ShadowClan, you will never be safe in the dark."

RIVERCLAN

Reedwhisker's Welcome

Intruders, Silverpaw? Are you sure? Oh, Onestar, it's you. What are you doing on this side of our territory? Great StarClan, that's a long walk for a pair of kittypets. Here, bring them down to the shore so they can cool their pads in the water. Are you joining WindClan? No? Then why . . . ?

I see. You want to know the secret behind RiverClan's strength in battle. Well, you are up to your bellies in it right now. That's right, *water*. Water feeds us, cools us, and keeps us safe from foxes, dogs, and curious Twolegs. It gives us the power to choose whether we fight or not, knowing that few cats are

brave enough to swim across our borders to attack us. Some say we are too quick to hide behind our barricade of streams, but it's easier to call us cowards than admit we have an advantage over all the other Clans.

We can slide out of rivers like fish with fur, silently flooding the shore before our enemy knows we are there. You may look at my Clanmates and see only sleek, glossy fur as thick as a kittypet's, but look closer and you'll find strong legs that can carve through water and tails that steer us through the swiftest currents.

Have you seen how we hunt? Not with speed or stealth or pounces, but with lightning reflexes, scooping fish from the lake while they drowse below the surface. How would you like to feel these claws raking over your spine? In close combat, RiverClan cats are the most feared among all the Clans because we can hold our enemy down and rake their bellies until they beg for mercy. If the ground is too open for close combat, we'll lure our enemies to the shore and drag them into the water to fight there. Other cats' fur quickly becomes sodden and heavy, pulling them down, but our fur sheds water like the feathers on a duck. We stay light and nimble, freed by the water rather than trapped by it. Our rivals don't stand any chance of winning when the lake fights alongside us.

So don't listen to the other Clans when they say we are proud, lazy cats who unsheathe our claws only to catch our food. They fear us because we have water as our ally. And because of all the Clans that ever lived in the forest or by the lake, we are the only one never to have been overrun against our will. *That* is real strength, young kittypets.

❀

Special Battle Tactic: The Rushpaw Splash

R iverClan *fish*! RiverClan *swim*! RiverClan warriors use water to *win*!"

The line of apprentices stopped chanting as they halted on the bank of the stream with their paws sinking into the soft brown earth. Mistystar looked proudly at them. She'd trained apprentices before, but being the RiverClan leader made her feel even more connected to these young cats who would fish and swim and fight to protect future generations.

"Into the water!" she called, and the four apprentices scrambled down the bank and waded into the gently flowing water.

"Ooh, it's cold!" whimpered Rushpaw, trying to stand on tiptoe to keep her belly fur dry.

Her littermate Tanglepaw snorted. "Don't be such a scaredy-mouse. You won't notice it after a while."

"That's easy for you to say," Rushpaw grumbled. "My legs are way shorter than yours. You're hardly wet up to your knees!"

Mistystar flicked her tail. "Rushpaw, would you like to run ahead and tell the enemy exactly where and when we're planning to attack? Perhaps you'd like to invite them to strike first?"

Rushpaw put her head to one side. "What would be the point of that? I thought you said we'd be learning about surprise attacks today?"

"That's what she's trying to teach us, fluff-brain," hissed Pikepaw. His dark gray fur bristled along his spine. "But you're making such a fuss that every cat from here to the mountains knows where we are!"

Rushpaw looked down at the surface of the stream and flattened her ears. "Oops. Sorry."

Mistystar tried not to let her amusement show in her voice. "Thank you for reminding us, Pikepaw," she meowed out loud. "Today we're going to pretend that this stream is the lake, and the far bank is the border of one of the other Clans. All the territories slope down to the shore, but you'll rarely find border patrols there because the other Clans don't see water as a point of access. Why does this give us an advantage?"

"RiverClan *fish*! RiverClan *swim*! RiverClan warriors use water to *win*!" the young cats shouted.

"Exactly. Now follow me, and make sure only your ears, eyes, and nose show above the water." Mistystar jumped down the bank and slid into the stream. The water flattened her fur, cold and comforting and lifting her gently off her paws. She let herself sink until only her muzzle peeped out, tipping back her head to keep her eyes and ears level with the surface. Pushing off with one hind paw, she let the current sweep her into the center of the stream, using long, graceful strokes to propel her between the banks.

The apprentices struck out behind her; twisting her head, Mistystar saw Pikepaw sink so far down that only the tip of his nose was visible. She hoped he could still see where he was going. Rushpaw and Tanglepaw's littermate Duckpaw held herself higher in the water, but she swam strongly, without splashing. Tanglepaw looked as if he were putting in more effort—probably because of his long fur, Mistystar guessed. It took a while for a RiverClan cat's fur to become glossy enough to shed water like a duck's feathers, and Tanglepaw would be weighed down as it became sodden. Behind him, Rushpaw paddled frantically as she tried to keep up; her legs were below the surface, but Mistystar could tell she was struggling, because her head bobbed from side to side and her tongue peeped out as she panted for breath.

The stream curved between banks shored up with tree roots and then opened out beside a broad, sandy shore. Mistystar used her tail to steer her toward the beginning of the shore and bent her legs as soon as her paws brushed the bottom of the stream, staying in a crouched position to slip quietly out of the water. "Follow me," she called over her shoulder. "I don't want to hear any of you leaving the stream!"

She stood halfway up the shore, facing inland, listening for her apprentices. A whisper of droplets told her that the first cat had emerged. That was fine; a border patrol would pay no attention to that. Heavier pads on the sand gave away Tanglepaw's exit, but masked any sound of Duckpaw. Now they were waiting for Rushpaw.

"Ow!"

The muffled yelp was followed by a splash. Mistystar spun around to see Rushpaw vanish headfirst under the water, then bob up almost at once, spluttering and thrashing with her front paws.

"I stubbed my toe on a stone!" she wailed.

Pikepaw curled his lip and Tanglepaw rolled his eyes. "Honestly, Rushpaw, you're hopeless!"

Rushpaw stumbled out of the water and stood on the sand, tilting back her head to glare at her brother. "I am not hopeless! I'm just a lot smaller than you!"

"If you're that small, maybe you should have stayed in the nursery," meowed Duckpaw. "You're spoiling everything!"

Rushpaw's tail drooped like a piece of wet fern. Mistystar stepped forward. "I would have made you *all* do the exercise again, anyway." She didn't want Rushpaw to get into trouble from her denmates because she had ruined their first exit. But Mistystar was beginning to have doubts about the undersized apprentice. RiverClan cats weren't known for their long legs, but Rushpaw's were shorter than most, and she didn't seem to have the serious attitude toward training that the other apprentices did. Should she go back to the nursery for a couple of moons to gain some maturity?

The apprentices paddled back into the stream and swam out to the center.

"I'm going to be an enemy patrol," Mistystar called. "See if you can surprise me upstream." She trotted across the shore and ducked into the undergrowth farther up the bank.

In the water, Tanglepaw took charge. "Let's swim ahead of her and set an ambush."

"The bank slopes down again on the far side of that willow

tree," mewed Duckpaw. "We can climb out there."

"Okay, but don't swim too fast," puffed Rushpaw.

"Perhaps you should stay here and keep watch in case she comes back?" Pikepaw suggested as he pushed off from the bottom.

Rushpaw splashed water at him with her front paw. "You're not leaving me behind! I'll get it right this time, I promise!"

Duckpaw circled around and swam alongside the little apprentice. "Don't worry; we won't leave you here. Just try to keep up, okay?"

"Er, I think we're supposed to be swimming silently?" Tanglepaw reminded them over his shoulder. He struck out, leading the group around a curve in the stream, toward the willow tree. He couldn't see Mistystar in the undergrowth that grew along the bank, and the noise of the water in his ears made it impossible to hear anything but the loudest birdcalls overhead. He just had to hope she was deep enough in the reeds that she didn't know how far the apprentices had swum.

A narrow strip of pebbly beach opened up as they passed the trailing willow branches. Tanglepaw steered into the cover of the delicate silver-green fronds and carefully lowered his paws to the bottom of the stream. The stones were larger here, and he took a moment to find his balance. Duckpaw, Pikepaw, and Rushpaw swam in behind him. They were enclosed in a pale green cave dappled with sparkles reflecting from the water and hidden from the bank by the trunk of the willow tree. It was a perfect place to launch an ambush.

A tiny crackle downstream revealed that Mistystar was approaching.

"Get ready," Tanglepaw whispered. "And remember, we can't make any noise as we leave the water."

Tanglepaw eased himself forward, placing each paw down

before he lifted the next. Pikepaw, Duckpaw, and Rushpaw kept close to him, easing through the branches toward the open shore. Out of the corner of his eye, Tanglepaw glimpsed a pale gray flash behind the willow tree. Mistystar was coming closer.

"Quick!" he hissed under his breath. Crouching low, he waded clear of the water, keeping his belly fur on the surface until most of the water had run off his fur. Pikepaw followed, then Duckpaw. But the she-cat moved too fast and sent back a small wave that slapped Rushpaw squarely across the muzzle.

"Ack!" she spluttered.

Tanglepaw froze. Behind the trunk of the willow tree, one of the shadows on the path stopped moving. Mistystar had heard the noise, too. She knew they were here; the exercise had failed!

Behind him, Rushpaw took another cautious step forward, as if she didn't know the task was already over. Her paw slipped off a smooth stone underwater and she stumbled forward. She flicked her tail as she tried to keep her balance, sending a glittering arc of droplets through the air to land with a splash downstream.

Tanglepaw was about to tell Rushpaw she was the clumsiest cat in all of the Clans, ever, when he realized that the shadow behind the willow tree had changed shape. It had whisked around, and he could see the outline of two pointed ears facing the other way, in the direction where the drops had landed. The splash had confused Mistystar into thinking the apprentices were downstream!

"Come on!" whispered Tanglepaw, leaping out of the water. In two swift bounds, he crossed the stones and leaped into the mottled shadows behind the tree. Mistystar spun around, her mouth open with surprise. She didn't have a chance to speak before all four apprentices bundled on top of her, claws sheathed, knocking her off her paws.

"Got you!" Duckpaw declared triumphantly.

"Did we pass the test?" Tanglepaw asked.

Mistystar pulled her muzzle free from Pikepaw's tail and puffed, "Yes! You passed! Now get off me!"

"Oh, sorry." Tanglepaw jumped up and gave the leader room to stand up and shake herself.

"Are you all here?" asked Mistystar, craning her neck to count them. "So who made that splash downstream?"

Rushpaw hung her head. "That was me," she mewed in a small voice. "I lost my balance and my tail flicked some water."

Mistystar stared at her. "It was a brilliant move! Making a noise downstream made me think you were somewhere completely different."

Tanglepaw nodded. "I saw from your shadow that you'd turned around, so I realized we could still catch you by surprise."

"That was very observant of you, Tanglepaw," Mistystar praised him. "Now, Rushpaw, do you think you could show us exactly what you did?"

Rushpaw blinked. "You mean I did something right?"

"Better than that," Mistystar told her. "You invented a brand-new tactic for water combat! And I think we'll call it the Rushpaw Splash!"

WATER COMBAT MOVES

RiverClan warriors have developed special techniques for fighting in the water. The water techniques are a closely guarded secret among RiverClan cats, so all training is done out of sight, along the streams that run through the territory.

DOUBLE-FRONT-PAW SLAP-DOWN: Splashes water into the face of the enemy.

UNDERWATER LEG SWEEP (FRONT OR HIND): The opponent will not see it coming under the water so won't have a chance to brace himself before losing his balance.

PUSH-DOWN AND RELEASE: Almost all non-RiverClan cats panic if they are submerged, while RiverClan cats know how to hold their breath underwater. This move can be used to secure a decisive victory, because it's most likely to make the opponent surrender.

UNDERWATER CLINCH: Uses warrior's weight to hold the opponent below the surface, with a firm grip that enables the warrior to bring his enemy spluttering back to the surface before forcing him under again.

TAIL SPLASH: Temporarily blinds opponent by flicking water in his eyes.

UNDERWATER PUSH-OFF: Crouching and erupting out of the water into opponent, using surprise and impact to knock him off balance.

RUSHPAW SPLASH: Using noise of water splashed at a distance to create a decoy, leaving opportunity for a surprise attack.

Hailstar Speaks: The Lost Kits

G reat StarClan, if what I am about to do is wrong, then send me a sign and the kits will stay where they are."

I tipped back my head and stared into the star-flecked sky. Silverpelt hung like a frosted cloud in the middle of the sky, an archway of ancient spirits leading to StarClan's hunting grounds. Nothing moved. StarClan had spoken with their silence: The mission would go ahead.

I drew a deep breath. I had known I would face challenges when I became RiverClan's leader, but this was beyond anything I had expected. For my Clan's sake, I could not fail.

I padded through the reeds to the warriors' den. The sound of breathing drifted on the cold air, with the scent of sleeping cats. Would they sleep so easily again after what I was about to ask them to do?

"Timberfur?" I whispered through the entrance.

A dark shape stirred inside, and Timberfur's head popped out. "Hailstar! What is it?"

"Bring Rippleclaw, Owlfur, and Ottersplash," I ordered. "Meet me outside the camp."

The big brown tom blinked; then his head vanished. I slipped out of the clearing and sat on the narrow pathway between the reeds. I could hear the river sliding past; was it whispering a warning?

The warriors appeared, shaking sleep from their heads and stretching their paws. Ottersplash looked worried, the white patches on her ginger fur glowing like snow.

"I want you to come to WindClan with me. We are going to take back Fallowtail's kits."

Four pairs of eyes stared at me in disbelief. Owlfur spoke first. "But . . . but you agreed that Reedfeather could raise them in WindClan."

Ottersplash nodded vigorously. "You said he had equal claim because he was their father, and RiverClan had enough mouths to feed this leaf-bare."

I pictured the WindClan deputy's glow of satisfaction as he led his daughters out of the RiverClan camp. Fallowtail had remained in the nursery, unable to watch. She knew she had broken the warrior code by falling in love with a WindClan cat; she was lucky that I had allowed her to stay in RiverClan after bearing his kits. There was no place for half-Clan cats in RiverClan. I wanted loyalty without question—I *deserved* it, because I was their leader.

But for the past moon I had watched Fallowtail slowly dying of grief for her lost kits. It was too great a punishment for her to bear.

"WindClan will expect this," Rippleclaw warned, breaking into my thoughts. "Heatherstar announced at the Gathering that they had doubled their border patrols."

"Not along the cliff," I replied. "I've been watching for the last three nights. If we approach from the gorge, we should be able to get to the camp without meeting any patrols."

"Then we're going to take the kits by force?" meowed Timberfur.

I looked at him without blinking. "You think Reedfeather would give them back if we asked nicely?"

Timberfur turned his head away, his gaze shadowed. I didn't allow myself time to wonder whether I was testing his warriors' loyalty beyond their limits. "Follow me," I ordered.

We walked in silence to the far border of their territory, where the wooden bridge crossed the river just after it spilled out of the gorge. The water stilled and flattened out in a matter of fox-lengths, as if it were exhausted by its maddened, foaming tumble between the high stone cliffs. On the far bank, a tiny path clung to the bottom of the stone, just above the water. If we could scale the cliff from there, we would be able to enter WindClan's territory along the unguarded border.

Owlfur padded alongside me as I crossed the bridge. "Did you tell Fallowtail what you were going to do?"

I shook my head. "She'll know when we succeed," I meowed.

The climb to the top of the cliff was harder than I'd imagined; our thick fur weighed us down, and Timberfur tore one of his claws when he lost his grip on a paw hold. Only Ottersplash giving him a shove from below stopped him from crashing all the way down to the bottom, where the river foamed over jagged rocks.

Finally we hauled ourselves, panting, over the edge of the stone wall and lay flat on our bellies, listening. Rippleclaw raised his head. "No scent of any patrols," he reported, keeping his mouth wide-open to taste the air. The breeze was blowing steadily from the forest, which would serve us well, bringing traces of any WindClan cats in that direction.

"Which way is the camp?" asked Ottersplash.

I tried to recall from my only previous visit, when I had been Heatherstar's guest. "In the center of the moor, I think. It's in a dip, so you can't see it as you approach, but there is a circle of gorse around the top."

Timberfur exhaled loudly. "So we're looking for some gorse bushes . . . on a moor."

"I never said it would be easy," I told him.

The brown tom flashed a look of anger toward me. "I didn't expect it to be. I'm a warrior, just like you are. Let's go." He strode away from the cliff, heading into the expanse of shadow that distinguished the moor from the night sky. We followed in single file, Owlfur at the rear. Ottersplash's white markings flared like starlight, and for a moment I wondered if it had been wise to bring her. Unlike the other Clans, WindClan hunted by sight, keeping watch for the flicker of movement that indicated a fleeing rabbit. Their patrols would be looking for intruders as well as listening and tasting the air. But we were deep into the moor now; there was no point sending Ottersplash back from here. Besides, we might need her.

Suddenly Timberfur froze. "Patrol dead ahead!" he hissed.

We flattened ourselves against the grass, feeling as exposed as rocks in an empty streambed. A small group of WindClan cats—no more than three or four—appeared briefly over a rise, then disappeared again as the ground sloped downward toward the forest.

"They didn't see us," breathed Rippleclaw. "Let's keep going."

Behind me, I heard Ottersplash take a deep breath and swallow. "There's stronger scent here. We must be close to the camp."

I peered into the darkness, trying to make out a circle of gorse. The moon was little more than a claw scratch in the sky, and the stars shed only the faintest light, so bushes and boulders showed up as patches of shadow against the dark bulk of the moor. But there was a line of bushes over to one side that looked more solid than the rest. Could they be sheltering the camp?

"That way," I hissed.

As we started forward, Rippleclaw asked, "What do you want us to do when we get there?"

"You and Timberfur deal with the guards while we find the

nursery. Ottersplash and Owlfur, you corner the queens, and I'll get the kits. Once I've taken them outside the nursery, Owlfur, you pick up one of the kits and we'll all make a run for it—but don't head back to the cliff. We can't carry the kits that way."

"Five of us against an entire Clan?" Owlfur mused. "We'll need to be lucky."

"We'll make our own luck," I told him grimly.

The sharp scent of WindClan grew stronger as we approached the gorse bushes. Pushing through the barrier, I stood at the edge of the shallow dip and looked down at the camp. More bushes screened scoops in the dusty soil that must have made rather drafty dens, and on the far side, a hawthorn tree with low-hanging branches enclosed a nest where the faintest squeaks and rustlings could be heard.

"That must be the nursery," I whispered, nodding toward the hawthorn.

Guards, Timberfur mouthed as two cats appeared at the rim of the hollow. He looked searchingly at me. "How much force do you want us to use?"

I knew what he was asking. I wasn't going to tell my warriors to break the warrior code—that had suffered enough already—but I wanted those kits back where they belonged. "Enough."

Timberfur nodded.

The guards were heading toward us but hadn't seen us yet. Timberfur and Rippleclaw turned and vanished back through the gorse bushes. A moment later, they slipped into view just behind the patrolling cats. Silently, and perfectly in step, they sprang onto the backs of the guards and rolled them into the gorse. Any squawks were quickly muffled; the bushes quivered briefly; then all was still. I pictured my warriors sitting heavily on the WindClan cats, keeping them quiet.

Lifting my tail to signal to my Clanmates, I raced down the side of the hollow and across the clearing to the hawthorn.

"Stop! Who's there?"

A yowl went up behind me; we'd been spotted. I nodded to Owlfur and Ottersplash, and they plunged through the branches of the hawthorn. At once the queens inside started shrieking and scrabbling to protect the kits. I spun around to face the cat who'd raised the alarm. It was Dawnstripe, her gold-and-cream-striped fur almost white in the starlight.

"Hailstar!" She gasped. "What are you doing?"

More cats were emerging from their dens around the hollow; there was no way any of them were going to listen to me. I whirled around and forced my way into the nursery. Inside was solid darkness, muggy and scented. "Ottersplash? Owlfur?" I hissed.

"Over here," Owlfur replied from the far corner. His voice sounded muffled, as if he were holding fur in his mouth. "The kits are with me."

There was a hiss and paws scrabbled against the earthen floor. "Let me go," spat the queen. "Those are WindClan kits!"

"Not anymore," I growled. Nosing forward, being careful not to tread on any small bundles of fur, I found Fallowtail's daughters. They were bigger than when I'd last seen them—of course—but they still carried her scent, and the touch of the fur reminded me of her softness. "Graykit? Willowkit? It's time to come home."

I picked one of them up and it let out a squeak.

There was a snarl from the opposite corner. "Put her down, or you'll regret it."

Ottersplash's paw landed on the queen's ear with a smack. "Those kits are ours, and you know it."

I couldn't reply because I had a mouthful of fur. I backed out of the den, shuffling the other kit under my belly with my front

paws. Hawthorn branches scraped my pelt; then cold air swept over my haunches. I turned around—and found a line of warriors facing me. Heatherstar stood in the center, her eyes fierce.

"You cannot steal our kits!"

I lowered the kit to the ground—I still wasn't sure which one it was—and met the WindClan leader's gaze. "They are RiverClan, too. They belong with their mother."

"They are my kits as much as Fallowtail's." A pale brown tabby stepped alongside Heatherstar. It was Reedfeather, the deputy. "You said we could have them!"

"I made a mistake." I forced the words out, choking as if they were thistles. "I've changed my mind."

"You can't do that," hissed Heatherstar.

There was movement behind me as Ottersplash and Owlfur emerged from the nursery. "He can," meowed Owlfur softly. "And we're here to help him."

"Three of you against all of us?" Heatherstar sounded scornful.

"Actually, there are five. And right now, I'd say we held the advantage."

Every cat, including me, turned to look up at the top of the hollow. Rippleclaw and Timberfur stood there with their unsheathed claws pressed against the throats of the guards.

"Let our Clanmates pass, or their blood will feed your barren home," Timberfur went on. The eyes of the guard he was holding bulged madly.

Heatherstar took a step back. Her gaze when it met mine was puzzled and a little sorrowful. "A threat to kill? That is not how we fight, Hailstar."

"It is when we have to," I replied through clenched teeth. I picked up the kit once more, and Ottersplash scooped up the other

"THE LOST KITS"

one. With Owlfur beside us, we carried them through the silent WindClan warriors and up the slope. Timberfur and Rippleclaw released the guards when we drew level; as the scrawny cats hurtled down the slope to their Clanmates, we pushed through the gorse bushes and started running for the border.

Thundering paw steps behind us told us that we were being pursued. I wasn't surprised; I would have done the same.

"Faster!" panted Rippleclaw.

The dark ground was a blur beneath my paws, and the kit wailed as she bumped against my legs. I tried to tip my head back to lift her higher, but she seemed to weigh as much as a full-grown cat, getting heavier with every stride. Owlfur tried to help me, but we couldn't match our pace and ended up falling over each other, sending the kit flying through the air. Timberfur snatched her up and we raced on. Behind us, the sky was growing lighter, and ahead I could see the dark line of the forest, then an empty gray space where the land dipped down to the river.

"That way!" I screeched, swerving.

The ground started to slope in front of us, lending speed to our paws. But the WindClan warriors hadn't already climbed up a cliff, and weren't burdened by kits. I could feel their breath on my tail, and a barb of pain shot through me as one of them reached out to claw my flank. I wrenched myself away and kept running without looking back.

"Get into the river!" I yowled to my Clanmates.

Ottersplash grabbed a mouthful of fur on Timberfur's kit, and Owlfur helped Rippleclaw with his. Side by side, the warriors raced awkwardly toward the water. I slowed down, offering myself as an easy target to our pursuers. At once I felt myself toppling over, crashing down on a rock, which sent a stab of agony along my ribs. Reedfeather stood over me, his lips pulled back in a snarl.

"You can't steal my kits!"

I looked up at him, wondering if I was about to lose one of my lives. "We already have!" I growled back.

Reedfeather raised his paw, ready to strike, when there was a screech from ahead. "They're nearly at the river!"

He dropped his paw and leaped away from me. "Stop them!" he ordered.

Letting out a quavering breath, I rolled over and pushed myself up. My warriors stood knee-deep in the water, facing the WindClan cats, with the kits placed on stones above the surface behind them. I charged across the grass, ignoring the pain in my side, and sprang on Reedfeather from behind, knocking him into the river. Cold water rushed up to enfold us in a noisy, bubbling grip. I threw back my head and took a gulp of air before thrusting down with my front paws as hard as I could. Beneath me, Reedfeather struggled to get free, sending up another flood of tiny bubbles. I unsheathed my claws until they pricked his skin beneath his thin fur.

All around me, my warriors wrestled with WindClan cats. Owlfur swept one of his paws and left one cat floundering out of his depth. Ottersplash dived down and surfaced under the belly of another warrior, sending him lurching off balance. Meanwhile, Timberfur and Rippleclaw swam to the far side with the kits and deposited them on the shore.

"Hailstar? Hailstar! Stop!"

Owlfur was standing beside me, wild eyed with fear. I looked down and saw Reedfeather's eyes beginning to close. His body hung heavily in my claws, and the bubbles were petering out. "You're killing him!" Owlfur hissed.

In horror, I unhooked my claws and stepped back. Reedfeather's body twitched in the current as he sank to the bottom. Owlfur pushed me back, ducked his head, and came up with the WindClan deputy hanging from his jaws. "Help me get him out!" he spluttered around a mouthful of sodden fur.

I grabbed the loose skin at the top of Reedfeather's tail and hauled him onto the sand. The deputy lay still for a moment while Owlfur rubbed his chest. Behind me, the other WindClan warriors stood frozen in horror. They knew they had lost the battle with us; now they were willing Reedfeather to win his battle with the river.

Suddenly Reedfeather bucked under Owlfur's paws and coughed up a stream of sticky water. He rolled onto his belly and coughed again.

"He'll be okay now," Owlfur meowed.

"No thanks to you," snarled one of the warriors, stepping forward. He glanced across the river to where Timberfur and Rippleclaw were licking the kits in an effort to dry them out. "I hope they were worth it."

I followed his gaze and thought of Fallowtail. "They are."

Shortly before Graypaw's sister, Willowpaw, was due to receive her warrior name, Fallowtail asked to speak to me in private.

"I'd like her warrior name to be Willowbreeze," she meowed. "And Graypaw to be Graypool. That way I'll always know that my daughters carry the strength of wind and water together."

I looked at her soft brown face, her blue eyes gazing earnestly into mine. She had never stopped loving Reedfeather, not for a single moment. I had won back her kits, but part of her heart lay on the moor, with the wind and the rabbits.

WINDCLAN

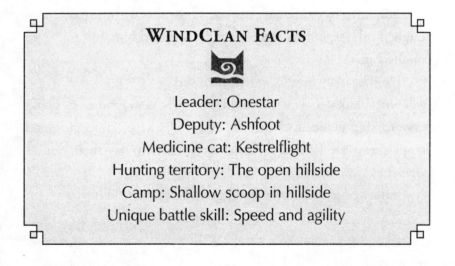

WINDCLAN FACTS

Leader: Onestar
Deputy: Ashfoot
Medicine cat: Kestrelflight
Hunting territory: The open hillside
Camp: Shallow scoop in hillside
Unique battle skill: Speed and agility

Ashfoot's Welcome

Welcome back, Onestar. I see your companions are still in one piece. They now know about three different kinds of combat—forest, water, and night. But they have yet to learn about WindClan's strengths, which enable us to survive on the bleakest, most open territory, where there is nowhere to hide from invaders, and where borders lie open to the sky, as fragile as the breeze.

Come into our camp, kittypets. That's right. Now settle down in the shade here, and help yourself to some fresh-kill. There are plenty of cats here with tales to tell you about battles from the past. See that dark gray tabby over there? That's Webfoot, our best storyteller. You'll have to squeeze past a crowd of kits to hear him talk!

You have nothing to fear here. Unlike the other Clans, who skulk in brambles or shadows or even in water, WindClan has nothing to hide. We live in the open, and we fight in the open, too, with two lines of cats facing one another across empty ground. This is surely the noblest way to fight. Both sides are equally prepared but only one Clan leaves the field victorious, in certain knowledge of its superior strength. The loser can only lick its wounds and accept that, this time, it fell short in strength, skill, or courage. Yes, the other Clans are content to skirmish amid bushes or mud, but as the great WindClan tactician Graywing the Wise taught us, it is open battles that carry the weight of destiny.

SPECIAL BATTLE TACTICS

Graywing the Wise led WindClan many, many moons ago, before "star" was added to leaders' names. He won the reputation for being the greatest leader of any Clan, thanks to his attention to battle strategy. He realized that the most important element of any battle was the position of warriors before and during combat. Using small stones and marks made by sticks on the floor of his den, he developed tactics for every sort of battle, even on WindClan's open moorland territory, where there were no natural hiding places or traps.

1. APPROACH FROM ABOVE YOUR ENEMY.

The advantage of gaining the higher ground is that you can charge at greater speed at the enemy, who will be weakened by having to fight uphill.

2. USE THE LIGHT FROM THE SUN.

The sun should be behind you to dazzle the enemy. In greenleaf, the midday sun is especially bright and cruel to cats who are used to skulking under the cover of trees. In leaf-bare, the low sun hovers around the eye line like a troublesome bee; keep your enemies facing it, and they'll have trouble seeing an attack from any direction.

3. KNOW WHERE THE WIND IS COMING FROM.

If there is a strong wind, it should blow from behind you toward the enemy, blinding them with dust and holding them back like the current of a river. If you wish to preserve the element of surprise, the wind should blow from the enemy position toward you so that your scent is carried away from them.

4. Conceal the Size of Your Force.

The number of cats in your battle patrols can be hidden to confuse the enemy from a distance. Cats packed tightly together will appear as a small attacking force, encouraging the enemy to be overconfident and make poor strategic decisions. Alternatively, if cats are spread out single file, they will look like a solid border of warriors, which will seem impenetrable to an advancing enemy.

5. Attack Both Ends of the Enemy Line First.

If both ends of the enemy's line are defeated, the cats in the center of the line will have to fight on two fronts. Even if they are not outnumbered, they will be outflanked, vulnerable, and in disarray.

6. Keep Fresh Warriors in Reserve.

Always have adequate reserves of fresh, fit warriors behind the battle line. They will be able to replace injured warriors, launch a separate attack if the enemy tries to encircle your forces, or fend off a surprise enemy from the rear. If the battle is in your favor, finish it by sending your reserve warriors behind the enemy line to surround them and demand surrender.

7. Feigned Retreat and Ambush.

A group of strong cats charges at the enemy, screeching, then turns around and withdraws. Repeat this until the infuriated enemy finally breaks its line and gives chase. Then the trap is sprung. Other warriors positioned in rabbit holes and in dips in the ground—out of the enemies' eye line—attack as soon as your opponents have gone past. The enemy will be forced to stop and turn around to fight this unexpected threat, and as they do the retreating cats must turn and charge back at them at full speed. The enemy is caught between two bodies of attacking cats and will quickly surrender.

Webfoot Speaks:
The Story of the Lost Tunneler

O kay, one story; then it's bedtime for all of you. I will tell you about a distant ancestor of mine, a young tunneler named Rabbittail who lived in the very early time of the Clans, before the Twolegs built the Thunderpath that cut ShadowClan off from the rest of the forest. Without the stinking trail of monsters to divide them, and with few clear territory markers on the empty hillside, WindClan and ShadowClan were forever bickering and squabbling about where the boundary should lie. Finally, after yet another ShadowClan patrol ignored WindClan's border marks, the two great Clans confronted each other on the moor for a deciding battle. Gorsestar, the WindClan leader, signaled to his Clanmates that they should use the feigned retreat and ambush against their crow-food-eating foes. Rabbittail, who was pale gray with a stunted white tail like a rabbit's, was one of the tunneling cats who crawled into a burrow, ready to attack the enemy as they crossed over his head. He figured that if he followed the tunnel farther down the hillside, he could come up on the far side of the enemy and attack them from behind at the same time his Clanmates appeared in the middle of their ranks.

As Rabbittail tunneled, he heard the WindClan warriors begin to charge and retreat above him, their paw steps echoing through the ground like thunder. But ShadowClan held steady, ignoring the insults hurled at them. Rabbittail kept going, right underneath the line of ShadowClan warriors. All at once, the

ground shuddered above him! The enemy had finally taken the bait and were charging after the retreating WindClan cats. Rabbittail twisted and turned along the narrow black paths, looking for one that would lead him up to the surface so he could launch his own attack. But he had never tunneled this far before, and the paw steps thudding overhead confused him until he knew he was walking in circles. Rabbittail was lost.

He forced himself to stand still in the cold, empty dark, and waited for his senses to tell him which way he should go. He felt a cool breeze stroke his flank, carrying a faint scent of rabbit. A breeze on its own could signify nothing more than a long, steep, unclimbable shaft reaching far underground; but combined with rabbit scent, it suggested that Rabbittail was close to the surface. He headed back the way he had come, staying quiet and scenting the air every few paces. The breeze on his face led him down a side tunnel, where the darkness began to fade to gray. He was nearly out!

Suddenly there was a scrabbling noise behind him, and an earsplitting yap bounced off the rock walls. There was a *dog* in the tunnels! Peering over his shoulder, Rabbittail caught a glimpse of brown-and-white fur, a pointed muzzle, and glistening black eyes before he pushed off with his hind legs and ran as hard as he could.

The tunnel twisted and turned, making him lose his footing more than once as he scrabbled to change direction. He could feel the dog's hot, stinking breath on his haunches, and flecks of saliva spattered over his back. But the gray light was growing brighter ahead of him, pulling him on and giving extra speed to his tired paws.

The sky burst open in front of him, and Rabbittail hurled himself out of the mouth of the tunnel, springing with all four feet off the ground.

But he didn't land with familiar prickly grass under his paws. Instead, he hung in midair, trapped in a floppy brown mesh that smelled strongly of Twolegs and rabbits. A furless pink face appeared beside him, shouting so loud that Rabbittail tried to shrink down in the net, but his hind paws slipped through the holes until he was swinging on his belly with his head twisted up at an angle. Behind him, to his horror, he saw a pile of dead rabbits, their necks broken. This was no tempting pile of fresh-kill: The Twoleg must have killed them when his dog chased them into the mesh.

Rabbittail was not used to giving up. He rolled onto his side and wrenched his paws clear of the mesh. Then he sank his claws into the coarse brown tendrils and ripped hard. One of his claws was torn out and blood sprang from his foot, making the dog circle madly on the ground below him. The Twoleg bellowed and shook the net, but Rabbittail clung on with his claws and hauled at the mesh until he felt it start to give way. He thrust down with his hind legs as hard as he could, and the mesh split open beneath him, spilling him onto the grass.

The dog pounced, but Rabbittail had already leaped up and was racing across the grass. He was on the far side of the moor from the camp, but there was a gully beyond the next rise that would lead him around the peak of the hill to just below the circle of gorse bushes that sheltered the dens.

For several long heartbeats, the dog chased him; Rabbittail considered whether he should find a burrow to hide in but decided that he might get lost again—and besides, the dog was small enough to follow him, as he had already found out. Just as he thought his legs would give way from exhaustion, the Twoleg shouted and Rabbittail heard the dog slither to a halt behind him. With a reluctant whine, it spun around and trotted back to the Twoleg.

Mouse-brained, fox-hearted, useless dog! Rabbittail thought as he skidded over the top of the rise and down into the gully. Gathering his paws beneath him, he headed for the camp, still running flat out. *You'd better hope that Twoleg lets you share his fresh-kill pile,* he thought, *because you're too dumb to catch your own prey.*

Well, I think that's enough. Bed, all of you! And when you wake up tomorrow, practice those battle skills. As the story proves, our battle skills serve us equally well in times of peace, giving us the strength and cunning to outwit Twolegs and dogs, and other creatures too dumb to know the skill of their enemies. Rabbittail never surrendered, and didn't let courage abandon him even when he was cornered by a dog in a place where dogs weren't supposed to be. Aboveground or in the tunnels, WindClan cats don't give up as easily as the other Clans think. There have been no easy victories against WindClan warriors, nor will there ever be.

Heathertail Speaks:
The Lost Skill of Tunneling

In the old territory, WindClan's moor was almost hollow with tunnels and burrows, some made by animals, others by underground streams that cut through stone and sand to leave endless holes filled with nothing but darkness. The cats who first settled there realized that the tunnels could be used to their advantage—not just for storing fresh-kill or sheltering from the weather, but as a strength against their enemies, enabling WindClan warriors to move right across their territory without being seen.

Certain cats—usually the smallest—were trained as tunnelers, clearing the secret passageways and memorizing the cobweb of paths that led underground. Some led right into other Clans' territories, giving a secret means of access into (or escape from) enemy camps; the exit was always carefully concealed with bracken and branches, and any trace of scent wiped away with the pelt of a freshly killed rabbit. Often the tunnelers grew so accustomed to working in blackness that they lost any daylight vision, and were clumsy and nervous above the ground. But once inside their tunnels, they could run as fast as any WindClan warrior, using scent and touch and sound to navigate their way beneath the entire forest.

Tunneling apprenticeships were keenly fought over—in spite of having to live in dark and cramped spaces for their working lives, tunnelers had special status among their Clanmates. Training took twice as long as for warriors, and injuries, even deaths, were common. A few hard-learned rules kept the most experienced tunnelers alive—and gave apprentices a chance to survive their first few moons below the surface of the moor.

They learned to leave a clear scent trail, marked like a border, so they could find a way out. They came to recognize the feel of the wind on their muzzles, knowing that it did not necessarily mean they were approaching the surface; shafts strike far underground, bringing fresh air to the lowest tunnels, but it is not always possible to climb up them. And even the least experienced tunneler stayed alert for the sound of dripping water—rivers are no place for WindClan cats, whether they're on the surface or belowground.

They learned to recognize the smell of underground animals, not to hunt them but to stay out of their way—no cat wants to end up in a den of foxes, and cornered rabbits can break ribs with their hind legs. After several moons of traveling below the surface, tunnelers were able to imagine their route aboveground, so they could keep track of where they were in the dark. This was the skill most highly prized among the Clan, because it was too easy to get lost in the darkness and vanish forever down a bottomless hole. These dark, secretive abilities were feared and respected by the tunnelers' Clanmates as much as by the other Clans.

When we settled by the lake, our tunneling skills were abandoned. "There are no tunnels here," declared the senior warriors. "All cats must be trained to hunt and fight aboveground from now on."

But some of us know differently. Some of us have explored and played and battled for our lives in the web of tunnels coiled below our new home. Cats in other Clans know our secret—Lionblaze, Jayfeather, and Hollyleaf. But it was all a terrible mistake. I should never have followed my curiosity belowground, out of the safety of daylight and fresh, clean air. I risked everything because I was in love with Lionblaze. But my discovery nearly carried us to StarClan—and the games we played ended up breaking our hearts.

SKYCLAN

SkyClan Facts

Leader: Leafstar
Deputy: Sharpclaw
Medicine cat: Echosong
Hunting territory: A sandy gorge
Camp: Caves in wall of gorge
Unique battle skill: Aboveground combat

Buzzardstar's Welcome

ello, kittypets. Don't be scared; you're asleep in WindClan's apprentice den, safe and well fed. My name is Buzzardstar, and I was once the leader of a Clan many days' travel from here. Even though I went to StarClan long ago, I can walk in the dreams of some cats. You are lucky that I can walk in yours, because there's one more Clan that you need to know about. Its name was SkyClan, and we were once the equal of any of the four Clans by the lake.

We earned our name because our warriors were happiest in the trees, hunting birds and climbing into nests for juicy, warm eggs. We could jump higher than any other cats, and climb more confidently, even to the thinnest branches. Like the hawks and eagles who swoop silently down on prey from above, SkyClan warriors could launch into battle from the air, dropping down on the enemy from the branches of trees and catching even the wariest intruders by surprise.

We were driven out of the forest many moons ago, when I was the deputy, after our territory was destroyed by Twolegs building new nests. We tried to make a new home at the source of the river that flowed through the forest, but we faced too many enemies, and within a few generations, my Clan had disappeared.

Even after watching the heartbreaking defeat of the Clanmates who came after me, I knew that SkyClan could live again, strong and proud and preserved by the warrior code. Cloudstar, the leader I had served under as a deputy, summoned Firestar from ThunderClan to find the descendants of the cats who had lived in the gorge and create a new SkyClan for their ancestors—my Clanmates and me—to watch over and protect. Now my Clan lives once more, relearning the old battle moves that moons ago made SkyClan one of the most respected Clans of the forest.

Special Battle Tactic:
Sparrowpaw Explains the Sky-drop

Clovertail? Clovertail, are you awake? Oh, good. I thought all those kits might have worn you out. Er, yes, they're lovely. Are they supposed to be that loud? Have they got a thorn stuck in them? They can't be hungry, surely! All they do is drink milk!

I think this one here's gone to sleep. Is that okay? Should I wake him up in case he's still hungry? I guess it would be nice for you if they all went to sleep. Okay, I'll leave him alone. Sorry, sorry! I didn't know his tail was right by my foot! Shhhh, little cat. It's all right; have some more milk. That's better. Where was I?

I wanted to tell you about this totally amazing battle move Sharpclaw taught me today. Apparently our ancestors—you know, the first SkyClan—used it all the time to defeat their enemies. Skywatcher told Firestar, and Firestar told Sharpclaw, and now he's going to teach all the apprentices! But he started with me, which must mean I'm the best, or the strongest, or the smartest, right?

Oh, yes, my new battle move. It's called the Sky-drop! Like something an eagle would do! It was just me doing it today, but usually it would be a whole bunch of warriors, called the drop patrol.

First I had to climb this really high tree. Then I had to wait on a branch, where I could see the path underneath in both directions.

Sharpclaw says that cats tend to look directly ahead or side to side—not up or down. So they don't realize there's a patrol right above their heads! SkyClan is so smart!

You don't just have to climb the tree quietly—which can be really hard when you get your paw stuck in a hole in the bark, let me tell you—you also have to be dead silent when you're waiting in the branches. You can't move a muscle, not even one little hair, in case that makes a leaf move. Do you have any idea how noisy leaves can be? When they're right by your ears, that rustling is like *thunder*! No wonder I couldn't hear Sharpclaw muttering down below. It was totally unfair that he got so mad at me. I am *not* as deaf as an old badger, so there!

And Sharpclaw says it's even harder to stay hidden in leaf-bare because there are no leaves to cover you. And if the sun's shining, then you have to remember that the enemy can see your shadow on the ground.

Today, Whitewhisker was pretending to be my enemy. So after I'd been waiting up there for about a *moon*, not breathing or *anything*, Whitewhisker walked along the path. When he was right underneath my branch, I let myself fall straight down, like Sharpclaw said—he wanted my belly to land on Whitewhisker's back so that I knocked him over. Later on I'll learn how to drop with my claws out, or ready to flick the enemy off his feet with my legs. And how to swing from my front legs to claw the enemy's face with my hind paws! There's no way we could lose a battle if we did that! I kind of wish there were some Clans living closer, just so we could be invaded. I'd be up the nearest tree, ready to squash them flat!

What? Oh, Whitewhisker's fine. I didn't actually land exactly where I was supposed to. You don't know how confusing it is to be up a tree, trying to balance on the thinnest branch you ever saw, and keep watching your enemy, and make sure you jump off at the right time. Sharpclaw says I was nowhere near Whitewhisker, but I definitely felt his tail brush against me. And that would be a pretty big shock for an invader, right? I bet it wouldn't matter if I didn't land on top of them. They might think it was raining cats! Splash! Splosh!

Oops. Sorry. Wow, for such stumpy little tails, they sure stretch a long way. Hey, can you believe they're still hungry? They must be all belly and nothing else inside! Well, good luck getting them back to sleep, Clovertail. They wake up really easily, you know. Maybe you should train them to sleep a bit more deeply? Okay, see you later!

Aboveground Battle Moves

It is a matter of great pride to SkyClan apprentices that they can carry out the Sky-drop, as well as these other moves.

> **THE SKY-CRUSHER:** Landing with all four feet on top of an opponent, flattening him like a leaf.

> **THE FLICK-OVER:** Landing with front paws outstretched to sweep the opponent off his feet and roll him onto his back.

> **THE KICK:** Kicking down hard as the warrior nears the ground, then using momentum from landing to spring away before the opponent can retaliate.

> **THE SLICE:** Dropping down with claws unsheathed for maximum injury.

> **THE BRANCH SWING:** Holding on to branch with front claws and swinging hind legs into the opponent's face.

> **THE REVERSE BRANCH SWING:** Holding on to branch with hind claws and striking with front legs through the swing.

> **THE TRUNK SPRING:** Sliding down trunk and springing off at head height, using hind legs to push off and clear opponents (good if tree is surrounded).

> **THE REVERSE CLIMB:** Climbing backward up the trunk as the opponent advances to gain advantage of height; often followed by Trunk Spring.

Cloudstorm Speaks:
A Lesson to Kittypet Thieves

Abattle against those mangy kittypets?" Nightfur's eyes gleamed, and he unsheathed his claws as if he were already imagining sinking them into glossy fur. The spine of a feather cracked under his front paw, and I looked down at the tattered remains of the plump thrush. It was inedible now, after the trespassers from Twolegplace had toyed with it and dragged it through the mud, not giving it the swift and respectful death that a warrior gives to its prey.

"They won't stand a chance against us!" Nightfur's apprentice, Fernpaw, agreed. "Once we drop out of the trees, we'll find out just how fast they can run—back to their precious Twolegs!"

I shook my head. "We can't fight them in our territory."

Buzzardpaw, an apprentice with a reputation for taking on warriors twice his size in battle practice without flinching, curled his lip. "How can you say that? Those kittypets ignore our border marks, chase off our patrols, and steal our prey. Are you suggesting we're too scared to defend ourselves?" he growled.

"Of course he isn't!" Birdflight, a she-cat who had been made warrior at the same time as me, jumped to my defense. "Cloudstorm is as brave as any of you—probably braver!"

I was grateful for her vote of confidence, but I didn't want our Clanmates thinking that I needed her to stand up for me. I blinked at her to say thanks, then got to my paws to address the gathered cats. "We know that the Twolegs are already uncomfortably close to our borders. We can tolerate them—but not their kittypets. These aren't fat, lazy, overfed creatures, but young, strong, bold cats who *catch* the birds we need for food, jumping high enough and fast enough to snag them in their claws and drag them out of the sky. They must have watched us train our apprentices in order to copy our hunting skills."

I noticed Petalfall, the deputy, widen her green eyes in surprise. As one of the youngest warriors, it wasn't my place to take charge of the Clan meeting. But she gave a tiny nod, so I carried on. I hoped she'd think my plan was good enough to report to Flystar when he returned from the Moonstone.

"We can't fight the kittypets in SkyClan because they don't all come here at once," I explained.

"If we scare a couple of them enough, they'll soon tell their thieving friends to keep away!" Nightfur interrupted.

"How do we know they talk to one another?" I argued. "They come from different Twoleg nests; they might not even know that other kittypets come into the woods, too. We need to take the battle to them. We must launch an attack on Twolegplace!"

There was silence. Then Fernpaw mewed, "What, *all* of it?"

"Of course not. Look." Using one of my foreclaws, I drew a line on the dusty ground. "This is the border between Twolegplace and our territory—it's a fence, right? About the height of a low tree, so we could still use a Sky-drop from it?" As my Clanmates shuffled closer, I drew some straight-edged shapes to represent Twoleg nests, with narrow paths between them. "We'll attack the kittypets closest to the fence first—on a sunny day they tend to lie in their own territories. After all, they don't *need* to hunt our prey for their food."

There were growls of agreement. Petalfall rested the tip of one claw on my dust marks. "What about the other kittypets? They don't all live underneath the fence."

"For those, we'll send patrols farther into Twolegplace," I meowed, tracing a line around the shapes on the ground. "Most of the little territories are enclosed with fences, and some have small trees that we can use to our advantage." I looked up and felt my heart pounding with excitement. "We'll show them we can fight as well in their territory as ours!"

"We'll invade Twolegplace!" Nightfur yowled. "This will be the greatest battle in SkyClan's history!"

We were ready at dawn the following day. Flystar hadn't returned from the Moonstone, but Petalfall agreed that we couldn't wait any longer. With every day that passed, we lost prey to our kittypet enemies. The air was warm before sunrise, promising the kind of hot, sleepy day that would keep the kittypets sprawled in their fussy, cramped territories. We set off through the trees in tense silence, four patrols, each with a different part of Twolegplace to attack. We'd start by lining up along the outer fence to deal with the kittypets who lived closest to the forest so that they couldn't send word to the others that they were under attack. Then we'd move into Twolegplace in four directions, using all the aboveground moves and warrior skills that defended our territory from other rivals.

Petalfall drew alongside me. Her rose-cream fur sparkled with dew, and the tips of her ears were dark with water as she brushed through the cool ferns. Her green eyes were worried, so I slowed my pace and steered deeper into the undergrowth, where we could talk without being overheard by the others.

"What's wrong?" I asked.

Petalfall blinked, as if she hadn't realized her thoughts were so obvious. "I think Flystar should know what we're doing," she meowed.

"He will, when we greet him with news of our victory," I answered.

"But what if StarClan has told him to do something else to deal with the kittypets? What if StarClan doesn't want us to attack them like this, in their own territory?"

I stopped and faced her. "Our warrior ancestors gave us the warrior code and the battle skills to protect and feed ourselves. They don't live among us, risking their fur to catch prey and drive out trespassers. These are things we must do for ourselves. We should be grateful for what they have taught us, but our actions are our own."

Petalfall took a step back. "But StarClan guides us in all things!"

"StarClan *watches* us," I corrected her. "That's different. It was my idea to take the fight into Twolegplace, not theirs. I hope we have their support, but our paws will carry us into battle, our claws will prove our strength to those thieving kittypets. This is our fight to win, not StarClan's."

Petalfall turned away, and for a moment I thought she was going to leave me there in the dew-heavy ferns and go back to the camp. I opened my mouth to ask her to stay—we'd need her skills and her courage—just as she paused and looked back at me. "I will fight alongside you," she meowed quietly. "And with StarClan's blessing, we will win. But if I were you, I'd be careful about dismissing our ancestors so lightly. We owe them everything, and it is a debt that will never be repaid."

The top of the fence dug into my belly as I lowered myself over, stretching my forepaws toward the ground and steadying my weight with the tips of my claws on the smooth, strong-smelling wood. I was aiming for a Trunk Spring to carry me over the thorny bush at the foot of the fence, leaving a clear run across the green grass to the kittypet sprawled under a tree on the far side. I heard fences creak on either side as my Clanmates eased themselves into position; one easy leap took us to the top of the fence, but our next move would be slow and careful, in order to take the kittypets by surprise. The slender wood underneath me wobbled as Birdflight lost her balance for a moment.

"Sorry!" she whispered from the territory beside mine.

I didn't reply, just sank one claw into the fence to hold myself still. From the other side came a low hiss. It was Petalfall's command to attack. The fences groaned as we pushed off with our hind legs and sprang into the Twoleg territories. My paws thudded onto soft grass and I crossed the distance to the tree in two bounds. The kittypet, a brown tabby with a flash of white on his chest, barely had time to lift his head before I pounced on him with my claws unsheathed.

"Wha . . . ?" he yowled. "Get off me!"

I cuffed his muzzle and jumped back as drops of blood scattered across my chest. "Stay out of our territory!" I snarled. From the other side of the fence, I could hear Birdflight hissing and spitting at the fat orange tom who'd stolen a squirrel in front of our hunting patrol three sunrises ago.

The brown tabby scrabbled backward, his eyes stretched wide. I tensed. There was something about the way he kept his hind paws tucked under him, the flex of his pelt as he gathered his haunches. . . . I was ready when he sprang, screeching in an echo of my own battle cry, raking the air with his outstretched claws. I flipped sideways, swiping his back feet from under him as I ducked away from his front paws. The tabby landed with a thud on the hard-packed earth. I stood over him and lowered my face until my muzzle was nearly touching his.

"Stay away from the forest," I hissed. "The prey is ours, and we can fight harder than this if we have to."

"Keep looking over your shoulder, fox-breath, because one day you might have to," the tabby grunted between clenched teeth.

I rested one paw on his throat and let my claws sink through his fur until I felt his skin flex beneath the thorn-sharp tips. "I could finish this now if you like," I offered.

The tabby winced, but to his credit, he didn't take his gaze from mine. "Those scrawny birds aren't worth fighting for," he growled. "You're welcome to them."

I lowered my paw and stepped back. The tabby sat up and blinked. "Is that it?" he mewed hoarsely.

I shook my head. "Only for you. Your thieving friends will be getting the same warning, wherever they are."

I spun around, racing for the gap at the side of the Twoleg nest that would lead me farther into kittypet territory. All around, I heard yowls of triumph from my Clanmates, and kittypet snarls abruptly cut off as the SkyClan warriors showed just how far we would go to keep our borders safe. When I burst onto the Thunderpath on the other side of the Twoleg nest, Birdflight and Buzzardpaw joined me, panting but bright-eyed with victory. I nodded to the ugly red nests across the hard black path. Side by side, we leaped forward to search out the next thief who would learn to leave the forest alone.

We won the battle, of course. Fired with hunger and fury after spending moons watching pampered kitties steal our prey, we dropped like hawks from trees and walls onto our startled enemies. We had the advantage of battle training as well as surprise; most of the time we barely needed to unsheathe our claws before the kittypets fled, or cowered in corners, begging for mercy. We stormed through Twolegplace, leaving no kittypet under the illusion that they would be welcome in the forest again. Some even pathetically offered to bring us their own food—as if we wouldn't rather starve than eat kittypet slop.

When Flystar returned from the Moonstone, he was relieved that we had secured our territory and made our prey our own once more. He summoned the Clan to thank the warriors who had taken the battle beyond our boundaries, and to order extra patrols for the next moon to make sure the kittypets stayed away. He said nothing about what StarClan had told him. Had they offered a different solution that was no longer needed? Or had they reminded Flystar that his Clan's strength lay in his living warriors, with sharp claws and hard-learned battle skills?

When Petalfall met my gaze across the camp, I lifted my chin, acknowledging what I had believed all along: that SkyClan's survival lay in our power, in the strength and swiftness of our paws, the thrust of our hind legs as we leaped higher than any other cat, and not in any dreams of warriors past.

PART TWO:
TOUR OF THE
BATTLEFIELDS

tbe lake
territories

✤

hello! My name is Tawnypelt. I'm a ShadowClan warrior.
Did you sleep well? Your fur seems a little ruffled. I expect
the sound of the wind might have disturbed you during the night.
Onestar has asked me to show you the places where battles have

been fought since we moved to the lake. We'll start here, on the moor. Did Onestar tell you that he had to fight for his own leadership as soon as Tallstar died? Every cat expected Mudclaw to take Tallstar's place because he was the WindClan deputy, but on the night Tallstar lost his ninth life, he changed his mind. No cat knows why—only Firestar and Brambleclaw were with him at the time—but he appointed Onewhisker deputy instead. Which meant that by dawn, he was leader of WindClan.

Mudclaw was furious—and can you blame him, really? He'd done nothing wrong. But as a warrior, he should have respected his leader's decision and supported Onestar. Instead, he plotted to take over WindClan by force, and visited all the other Clans in secret, gaining allies. They struck one night, Mudclaw and a RiverClan warrior named Hawkfrost leading the attack. The rest of us fought on Onestar's behalf, and Onestar won—helped by StarClan. Do you see that island down there? With the tall trees? If you look closely, you can make out a fallen tree joining the island to the shore, with its roots on the island side. StarClan sent a bolt of lightning to strike that tree and make it fall on top of Mudclaw, killing him instantly, and showing that Onestar was the true leader of WindClan.

Come this way, along the shore toward ThunderClan's territory. Every cat has the right to walk within three tail-lengths of the water all the way around the lake. If you look through the trees, you might just catch a glimpse of a Twoleg nest. It's falling down now, but there's an old Thunderpath that leads to it, and beyond to the hollow where ThunderClan cats live. The biggest battle since we came to the lake took place here. It started with a border dispute between WindClan and ThunderClan; then the other Clans got involved, and we fought for three days. ShadowClan fought on the side of ThunderClan—that's an

alliance that hasn't happened very often!

It was terrible, fighting cats who I'd shared tongues with at Gatherings, or fought alongside in other battles. But that's what being a warrior is all about—being ready to fight for your Clan whenever you have to. You just have to focus on your battle skills, think about what will be achieved or saved by winning, and get on with it. Some cats enjoy it; others see it as their duty.

We're getting close to the ShadowClan border now. Before we cross it, follow me down to the edge of the lake. There isn't a path, but we can walk along this gully. If you duck under that fern, you'll be able to stand on a strip of pebbles right beside the water. It's a great view of the lake, but that's not why I've brought you to this part of the shore. One cat who enjoyed battles too much, in my opinion, died here. So much blood flowed out of him that the lake turned red. The prophecy came true: "Before all is peaceful, blood will spill blood, and the lake will run red." It's okay; you don't need to look so horrified that your paws got a bit wet from that wave. The blood's all washed away now.

The dead cat's name was Hawkfrost, and if you must know, my brother Brambleclaw killed him, to save Firestar's life.

Now, hurry up and we'll go to ShadowClan's territory. Can you walk a bit faster than that? We don't want to get spotted by Twolegs while we're crossing this stretch of grass. ShadowClan and ThunderClan fought over this not long ago; sometimes I think I can still smell blood in the air. Firestar gave us this strip of territory soon after we came to the lake, then changed his mind and demanded it back. As if we'd give it up without a fight! The battle ended when Lionblaze killed Russetfur, our deputy. Warriors should never kill one another for the sake of victory. Neither side won that day.

Most battles are settled more easily, thank StarClan. There were some kittypets living here when we arrived who learned to respect us the hard way. They kept stealing our prey, invading our camp, even lying in wait for our apprentices. Stupid mouse-brains, did they really think they could take on the whole of ShadowClan? We took the battle to their own territory, a Twoleg nest in the middle of the trees, just beyond that rise. They fought well, for pampered kittypets, but they were never going to win.

The kittypets keep out of our way now, but we don't trust them, and our hunting patrols stay away from the Twoleg nest. There are plenty of other places to find prey. No, not here, there's no cover. See how the trees finish and hard black stone covers the ground? This is where Twolegs come in greenleaf to float on the lake. On the far side, where those bushes are, is the start of RiverClan's territory. They've fought their own battle there, against young Twolegs who tried to take over their camp. I heard the warriors made the river wider to protect their dens! Only RiverClan would fight back with water.

It was the same in the old territories, before we came to the lake. You've heard the Clans used to live somewhere else, right? Back then, RiverClan's camp was on the bank of a river, too broad to jump across except in the driest greenleaf. All the fighting was done on the other side of the river, where the rest of the Clans lived. Our territories there weren't so different from the ones we have now—WindClan lived on a moor, ThunderClan among the thickest trees, and ShadowClan in a copse of pines, surrounded by marshland. It's all gone now, crushed and splintered into the mud by Twolegs. All those battles that were fought, the borders we once defended with our lives, the dens where warriors were born and trained, have been lost forever. Good memories as well as bad, fading in the sunlight like dew. I'm sorry you won't get a chance to see those territories, too.

Great StarClan, where did all this mist come from? I'd better get you back to WindClan's camp before we get lost. Come on, follow me.

tbe fOREST
tERRItORIES

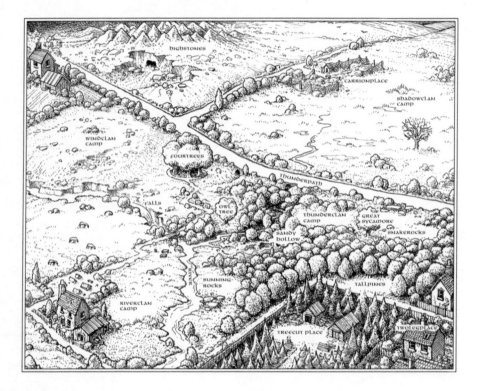

✳

bello, kittypets. You're a long way from home, aren't you? Do you know who I am? I'm sure that you've heard my name, even though no cat would expect you to meet me. I am Tigerstar, once warrior of ThunderClan, then leader of ShadowClan. Now

I walk in the Place of No Stars, the Dark Forest where cats with courage and ambition and cunning are sent, denied entry to StarClan by cats who see no farther than the end of their own noses.

There's no use calling to Tawnypelt. She can't see me; I've come only for you. There's something I need to show you. Tawnypelt was wrong when she said you would never be able to visit the old territories of the Clans. Come this way, through the mist.

That rustling noise? It's the branches of the four Great Oaks, one for each of the Clans. Look up; can you see them? Yes, we are in the forest, as it once was. This is the hollow where the Clans gathered every full moon—and it's the place where I lost every one of my nine lives, ripped from my belly by that traitor Scourge. Not long after, the Clans fought their greatest battle against Scourge and his followers, who called themselves BloodClan. I should have fought alongside my Clanmates! Instead I could do nothing but watch as the cat who had promised to help me take over the forest waged war against the Clans. They lined up at sunrise here, under the trees looking down into the hollow. Firestar led out the Clans from the other side of the hollow. Can you imagine how puny they looked? If you'd been standing here beside Scourge, you would have had dog claws fitted over your own, and the scent of blood and victory in your throat. You'd just seen your leader kill *me*, the greatest warrior of all the forest Clans; the other warriors must have looked like easy prey.

Just by this rock is where Whitestorm, the ThunderClan deputy, was killed by the BloodClan cat Bone. ThunderClan apprentices avenged his death, jumping onto Bone and dragging him down, clawing the life out of him. Even in the Place of No Stars I could hear his screams, and their shrieks of victory. StarClan never would have let Scourge win that battle. And Firestar showed great courage; I'll grant him that. He'll need every last whisker of it when we meet again.

Are you shivering from cold or are you scared? Stand close to me—it's all right, I bite only my enemies. It's colder now because we're on the open moorland, where WindClan used to live. Looks like their territory by the lake, doesn't it? You can see why they're so skinny and fast, when they have to chase rabbits all the time. Foolish cats, they should learn to stalk and pounce; then they could find fresh-kill under cover of trees. Come to the edge of the camp, in this shallow dip. Can you believe they chose to make their dens here? No wonder ShadowClan forced them out. Brokenstar defeated them with a single patrol, rushing down into the hollow and trapping the WindClan warriors in their nests before they realized what was happening. It was a classic ShadowClan ambush—but in the enemy's own den. Tallstar didn't bring WindClan back to the moor until Firestar and Graystripe fetched him. Firestar has been criticized a lot for constantly interfering in WindClan's affairs, but if Tallstar hadn't shown such weakness against Brokenstar, his Clan never would have gotten so reliant on ThunderClan's help.

Jump! Come on, just one more leap and you'll be on top of Sunningrocks. Look at the view! You can see the whole forest from here; those dark trees in the distance are where ShadowClan lived, and the harsh orange lights over there come from Twolegplace.

Feels peaceful up here, doesn't it? But these rocks have been the site of more battles than anywhere else in the forest. RiverClan would never accept that Sunningrocks belonged to ThunderClan. As if those fat, lazy fox-hearts didn't have enough places to lie in the sun. It's not like they could catch prey on the rocks, since they wouldn't know what to do with a mouse if one sat on their paws. Battles here were *boring*. Whichever cats had the highest place on the rock would win, simple as that. You can't escape when warriors are dropping like rain on your shoulders.

But there was one battle, not long before Firestar joined the Clan, where these rocks served me well. See that gully down there? Ah, that's better; now we can walk through it. Squeeze past the rock shaped like a cat's muzzle. Here, in this space so narrow that it's almost like a cave, I watched my deputy, Redtail, kill Oakheart, the RiverClan deputy. It was a quick fight—Oakheart tried to use his weight to knock Redtail against the stone wall, but Redtail sprang right over him, reaching down to slice Oakheart's flanks with his claws. Oakheart staggered and crashed onto his knees; he tried to lash out at Redtail, who just stepped backward, knowing the fight was over as Oakheart's life spilled out onto the sand. In that moment, I saw the best opportunity I'd had to make deputy. I was a good warrior; I *deserved* to be deputy. Only Redtail stood in my way.

Look up; see how tight the gully is above our heads. I knew that no cats elsewhere on Sunningrocks would have seen what just happened. The truth about Oakheart's death could die with Redtail. My Clanmate thought I was going to congratulate him. He never saw the strike that fell across his neck. He lay where you're standing now with the light of victory still in his eyes. I carried his body back to the camp and told Bluestar that Oakheart had killed him, and I had taken Oakheart's life in furious vengeance. I should have been made deputy! Not Lionheart! Bluestar knew nothing of justice and true courage!

I had my revenge seasons later, when I became leader of ShadowClan. Dogs came to the forest, fierce and wild and ravenous, and I turned them on my former Clanmates to show they should never have doubted my loyalty. Look around—we're not at Sunningrocks now. This is Snakerocks, a place where few hunting patrols come because of the adders that live here. But ThunderClan had far more to fear when the dogs made a den in a cave under that overhanging slab of rock. I kept the dogs here by bringing them fresh rabbits; it was easy to sneak into ThunderClan's territory when my scent was not fully ShadowClan. The first victims were apprentices, Brightpaw and Swiftpaw, who were foolish enough to hunt too close. Swiftpaw was killed at once; Brightpaw survived, but she has probably wished more than once since then that she hadn't. Did you see her in ThunderClan? The cat with half a face?

If I'd had my way, the dogs would have invaded the ravine, lured there by my trail of rabbits, and destroyed ThunderClan forever. I misjudged the courage of my old Clanmates; I should have known they'd treat this as one more battle, protected by their faith in their precious StarClan. Firestar, who was deputy by then, arranged a line of cats to lead the dogs away from the camp.

We're at the top of the ravine now—look down there, where the bushes are thickest. Our dens were hidden around a clearing; if the dogs had made it that far, the cats would have been trapped by the brambles they had relied on for shelter and protection. Ashfur and Ferncloud ran first, because they had lost their mother, Brindleface, to the dogs. They raced through the trees with the dogs on their heels; then Sandstorm took over. One by one, ThunderClan warriors led the dogs through the trees to the gorge. Do you hear that sound like thunder? That's the river churning along the foot of the cliffs at the edge of WindClan's territory. Bluestar gave up her ninth life to lure the dogs over. In our final battle, she won. She saved her Clan and secured her place in StarClan.

Stay away from the edge! You don't want to follow Bluestar, do you? It's time I took you back to Tawnypelt. I can hear her calling through the mist. Oh, I wouldn't tell her that you saw me if I were you. She may be my daughter, but she's like most of the other cats by the lake, who view courage in battle as something not to be trusted. Ha, if any of them had a whisker of my ambition, none of the leaders would sleep in peace! I have no regrets—everything is turning out as I planned—but I miss those days in the forest, when battles answered all the questions, and my allies would shed every last drop of blood fighting alongside me.

PART THREE: FAMOUS BATTLES

The Gathering

What do we have here? *Kittypets?* At a *Gathering?* Ah, Onestar, they're with you. That's all right then, I suppose. Make yourselves comfortable—no, not there! That's Pouncetail's favorite spot. Come sit beside me on this log. My name's Dapplenose; Pouncetail and I belong to RiverClan. Over there are Cedarheart, Tallpoppy, and Snaketail from ShadowClan. Don't take any notice of them; they're always making faces. I could outrun them when we were all warriors, so they don't scare me. Yes, I could, Snaketail! The brown she-cat is Mousefur from ThunderClan. I haven't seen her at Gatherings for many moons, poor old thing.

Her denmate, Longtail, died last moon when a tree fell into their camp. Treat her gently, if you speak to her. The bitter scent that clings to her is grief.

The last battle I fought in? It was when all four Clans met in ThunderClan's territory. Not a proud time for any of us. Did you hear how StarClan stopped it? *They made the sun disappear!* Terrible, terrible. We thought the world was coming to an end. Even after the sun came back, we were scared for a long time that it would vanish again. If you can't trust the sun to be in the sky, what can you trust?

But not all of that battle was shameful. Pouncetail will tell you the story if you ask him nicely enough. He was pretty much the only cat who brought honor to RiverClan that day. . . .

Ah, I see Nightwhisper is here tonight. See that scrawny brown tom under the thorn tree? He has a tale that will haunt your dreams, if you dare to listen. I've heard from his Clanmates that his sleep is haunted, and he wakes shrieking about rivers of blood and the taste of enemy fur in his mouth. He has seen too many battles alongside Tigerstar, I fear.

But not all of our battles were against other Clans, you know. We have united more than once against a common enemy—there was even a time back in the forest when foxes caused so much trouble, it took all four Clans to drive them out. Maybe Graystripe will tell you about that later. Listen well, young kittypets. The history of our Clans is alive around you, preserved in the memories of every cat.

Pouncetail Speaks: A Time for Mercy

I was doing my duty according to the warrior code; that's all,
Dapplenose. But you're right; a lot of us forgot about compassion
that day. We came in support of WindClan, believing they had been
treated unfairly over their recent border dispute with ThunderClan.
The battle was like a roaring lion by the time we reached the shore
below ThunderClan's camp; we could hear it echoing through the
trees, and followed the trails of blood to where cats from the other
three Clans wrestled and sliced and spat.

I wasn't afraid. I was a warrior: This was what I had been
trained for from the moment my eyes first opened. I didn't know
ThunderClan's territory well, but my Clanmate Blackclaw had
visited the hollow once with Mothwing, our medicine cat. He
told us about an abandoned Twoleg nest that would give us the
advantage of height as well as a place to lie in wait for other cats
passing along the old Thunderpath. We crept through the bracken,
skirting the hollow, fighting not to get tangled up in the wretched
undergrowth.

At last we crawled out onto a broad stone track speckled
with weeds—the old Thunderpath, I guessed. I shook myself,
convinced that I'd left half my pelt stuck on brambles. Blackclaw
and Reedwhisker had emerged a couple of tail-lengths away on
one side; on the other, Dawnflower scrambled out, hissing at a
tendril that was trailing after her, stuck to her tail. I ran over and
trod on the tendril, letting her pull herself free.

"This way," Blackclaw called in a low voice.

We slunk along the edge of the path, keeping as close to the undergrowth as we could without getting tangled. The sound of fighting came from behind us through the trees as my Clanmates leaped bravely to help WindClan against a patrol of angry ThunderClan cats. Ahead, the stone track was quiet—too quiet. The scent of ShadowClan hung on the breeze, growing stronger as we crept forward.

Blackclaw stopped in the shelter of some ferns that were straying onto the path. "The Twoleg nest is just beyond here," he whispered.

"I don't like this silence. I can smell ShadowClan close by," Reedwhisker growled.

Dawnflower nodded. "They could be using the nest for an ambush of their own."

"Then we'll attack as if we expect them to be there," Blackclaw decided. "If the nest turns out to be empty, so much the better. Pouncetail, you and Reedwhisker go around the back." He pointed with his tail. "If I remember correctly, there's a hole halfway up the wall that you should be able to jump through. Dawnflower and I will take the front entrance."

Beside me, Reedwhisker was breathing hard, his claws sinking into the leafy dirt between the cracked stone. I kept my claws sheathed and stared into the undergrowth that blocked my view of the Twoleg nest. I thought I could see a tiny path leading through, perhaps made by a rabbit or a mouse trundling in search of food.

"Go!" hissed Blackclaw.

I sprang into the bracken, aiming for the almost invisible trail, with Reedwhisker at my paws. Picking up the scent of mouse, I weaved through the stalks where tiny paws had walked ahead of me, trying not to shudder as fronds clutched at my pelt.

Suddenly the air ahead dazzled me with light, and I stopped just before I burst into the open. Peering cautiously out, I saw the Twoleg nest, which looked more like a pile of stones crumbling to the ground. There was no sign of any cat, but ShadowClan scent clung to the warm breeze amid the sickly smell of dusty leaves and churned-up bracken. We padded over to the Twoleg nest and waited under the hole in the wall that Blackclaw had described.

Faint murmurs came from inside: "Can you see anything?"

"No, but I'm sure I heard a RiverClan cat yowl just now."

"Have they come to help WindClan, do you think?"

"They wouldn't have had to come all this way to help ThunderClan, would they, mouse-brain? They'd have attacked WindClan from the other side!"

"No point ruffling our fur about RiverClan," put in a third voice. "That bunch of fatties wouldn't take on a mouse if it lay down under their paws."

I used my tail to tell Reedwhisker to get ready. When I flicked the tip, we both sprang up to the hole, scrabbling against the rough stone with our hind legs to push ourselves up. I balanced on the narrow wall, blinking to let my eyes adjust to the darkness inside the nest. Three pairs of eyes stared at me in surprise. Before they had a chance to react, I howled, "Attack!" and jumped down into the nest.

I stumbled as I landed on the pitted earthen floor, and a ShadowClan warrior flung himself onto my back. I let myself keep falling until I was rolling sideways, sending the warrior right over me. I jumped to my paws and spun around to face the small, pale-colored she-cat; the name Whitetail flashed through my mind, but this wasn't a Gathering. Individual warriors don't matter in a battle. Only winning matters.

I waited for her to launch herself at me, then dodged away

and flicked my front paw into her face. It was kind of like catching a fish—but with a much easier target. ShadowClan cats are like great, hairy boulders compared with a swift flash of trout! Whitetail screeched and staggered back, bleeding from her nose. Blackclaw was waiting for her, and bit her flank so hard that she left a clump of fur in his teeth as she wrenched herself free and fled.

Reedwhisker was wrestling with a ShadowClan tom in a corner—it was you, Snaketail, wasn't it? You fought well, my old friend, and I'll admit that Reedwhisker got lucky when you hit your head on that lump of stone and gave him a chance to pin you down. The third ShadowClan cat was a brown tom called Antpelt, who'd threatened me at the previous Gathering just because I scolded his apprentice for being rude to an elder. I don't mind telling you that I relished the chance to get even with him. Blackclaw and I forced him through a gap in the wall into another den, this one smaller and darker than the first. It was hard to spot his dingy pelt in the shadows, but he gave himself away by squeaking like a kit when something scrabbled in the corner—a rat, by the smell of it. Blackclaw and I pounced on the ShadowClan warrior, and thumped his ears until he dashed to the front entrance, still squealing.

We had captured the Twoleg nest! A jagged wooden slope led up to the rafters of the nest and I ran lightly up, disturbing the thick gray dust with my paws so that motes hung sparkling in the shafts of sunlight that pierced the broken roof. I paced along the nearest length of wood and looked out of a gap beneath the roof. I had a clear view of the Thunderpath in both directions. Blackclaw was right: This place was perfect for an ambush!

Suddenly there was a screech from below. I looked down through the slats of wood and saw my Clanmates advancing on a cat who seemed to be trying to bury himself in a corner of the nest. It was a ShadowClan warrior, but so streaked with dirt and blood that I couldn't tell which one.

Dawnflower looked up. "This one was hiding in here like a coward. His Clanmates won't thank him for leaving them to face us alone. Shall we teach him a lesson?"

The cat stared up at me, his blue eyes huge and pale against his filthy pelt. His mouth opened, but only a tiny hoarse cough came out.

Reedwhisker raised his paw and held it over the cat's neck. "Shall I finish him?" he offered. "Or do you want to have that pleasure, Pouncetail?"

A broken piece of wood sloped down to a heap of stones at the side of the den below me. I padded down the wood, sinking in my claws to stop myself from sliding onto the heads of my Clanmates. As I jumped onto the floor, they stepped back from the ShadowClan cat, giving me the honor of claiming this victory. I walked over to the quivering warrior. He was young, perhaps only a moon or two beyond his apprentice days. Beneath the dirt, his fur was gray, and his front paws were black.

"You're Spiderfoot, aren't you?" I snarled, recognizing him.

The tom nodded.

"Stand up," I ordered.

Spiderfoot hauled himself to his feet, stumbling on a piece of stone. I nodded to the sloping piece of wood. "Walk up there."

Still looking

terrified, Spiderfoot jumped over the fallen stones and clawed his way up the beam. I followed.

"Ah," growled Blackclaw, sounding satisfied. "Going to see if he has wings instead of the courage of a warrior, are you? Good idea."

Spiderfoot reached the gap underneath the roof and stared at me. "Are you really going to push me off?" he whimpered.

Feeling queasy at his sharp-scented fear, I shook my head. "Not this time." I twitched my ears toward the jagged slope of wood that led down to the entrance of the nest. "Go back to your Clanmates," I told him. "And warn them not to underestimate RiverClan warriors again."

Spiderfoot gazed at me for a moment more, as if he couldn't believe I was letting him go, just like that. Then he spun around and fled, leaving deep scores in the dust.

I followed him more slowly down to the floor of the nest. Blackclaw, Dawnflower, and Reedwhisker were waiting for me with their mouths open.

"You missed a chance to show ShadowClan just how fierce RiverClan can be," Blackclaw spat.

I looked steadily at him. "The warrior code says that we do not have to kill to achieve victory. Having mercy on your enemy, and sparing him to fight another day, shows the greatest courage of all. Where is the honor in winning four against one?"

I padded toward the entrance. Already I could hear more cats approaching. "Come," I meowed to my Clanmates. "One battle has been won, but the war is not yet over."

Nightwhisper Speaks: A Rogue's Story

I was born in the Twolegplace beside the forest where the Clans used to live. My mother was a stray, and never spoke of living with Twolegs, although her coat was soft enough that it wasn't hard to imagine she had once lived in a red stone nest and been a plump, spoiled kittypet. My littermates and I learned to fight by doing battle with one another amid the looming walls and bright green grass of Twolegplace, keeping out of the way of dogs and other cats, coming out only at night, when the alleyways were quiet and empty.

By the time I was full-grown, two of my brothers had been killed on the Thunderpaths, and my sister had chosen to live with Twolegs. I saw her sometimes, sprawled on flat white stones outside her housefolk's nest, or licking her plump belly, her fur stinking of kittypet slop. I was left alone, stealing food from Twoleg scraps, hiding from cats who would have ripped my pelt off for the sake of a chicken bone. Some cats talked to me, when we all had full bellies or were too weak with hunger to fight. They told me that they were exiles from ShadowClan, chased out of their home for breaking the rules of the warrior code. They told me about how the code had once kept them safe and strong and bound in loyalty to the cats who shared their territory. I envied those cats, and secretly thought the exiles were fools to have thrown away what they had before.

Then another cat came to the Twolegplace. Tall, dark furred, with muscles rippling across his wide shoulders. "My name is Tigerclaw," he told us. "And I need your help."

He came from a different territory from the exiled cats, one that belonged to ThunderClan. The current leader, Bluestar, was weak, and as her deputy, Tigerclaw stood to take over if she died. Bluestar was also holding a brave and noble cat prisoner—ShadowClan's former leader, Brokentail, who had once been the most feared cat of all the Clans but was now blind and wretched.

"Join me," Tigerclaw urged. "Fight beside me, kill Bluestar, and ThunderClan will look to us to lead them instead. Brokentail will be honored as he should be, and we will make our Clan stronger than any other. Our new Clanmates will thank us for getting rid of their frail and mistrustful leader, and we'll have food and shelter for the rest of our lives." As he spoke, his burning amber eyes rested on me, and I felt my fur tingle.

"The cat who kills the flame-colored warrior Fireheart will have a special place in my Clan. Destroy him, and you will walk beside me as my deputy."

I felt as though I had finally come home. I could be a warrior, protecting my Clanmates, serving my leader, earning his respect by getting rid of the cats who weakened our Clan and made our territory vulnerable. I would kill Fireheart!

We ran through the forest, thirsty for blood, bristling with rage against this foolish Clan that clung to their failing leader like moss to a rotten tree. Tigerclaw led us along invisible trails through the undergrowth; brambles raked my ears, but I didn't care, not even when the salty tang of blood flicked against my muzzle. I would shed more blood than this to fight for Tigerclaw!

Suddenly the ground dropped away in front of us, and Tigerclaw plunged into a ravine that seemed to be full of nothing but prickly bushes and a few smooth gray boulders. We thrust our way through a tunnel of gorse behind him, and burst out into a sandy clearing, circled by bushes that smelled strongly of cats. Faces popped out around us, wide-eyed with horror.

"Invaders!" screeched a she-cat, spinning around and diving back into a clump of brambles. I eyed the savage thorns warily, and decided not to follow. More cats leaped out of the undergrowth, sleek and shiny and strong. *These must be ThunderClan's warriors,* I thought. *But there's only one I'm interested in.*

I scanned the clearing for a cat the color of flame. Only tabbies and shades of brown stood out against the green branches.

"ThunderClan! Enemies! Attack!" yowled Tigerclaw, and to my astonishment, he sprang at the cat who had run closest to him through the forest and wrestled him to the ground.

Was it a trap? Had he lured us here to ambush us with his Clanmates? What had we done to them to deserve this?

Then I realized that the cat sprawled beneath Tigerclaw wasn't shrieking in pain; in fact, Tigerclaw's paws were round and smooth, claws sheathed, and when he bit down on the cat's neck, he curled his lips over his sharp teeth. This must be part of the plan! Tigerclaw wanted his Clanmates to believe that he was fighting alongside them!

All around me, the cats from the Twolegplace grappled with Clan warriors, yowling and spitting and slashing with their claws. On the far side of the clearing, a massive black tom with clouded eyes jumped onto the back of a small dirt-colored cat and started battering his ears. *That must be Brokentail.* I started to go over to help, but stopped when a flash of orange caught my eye. I spun around and stared at the ginger tom leaping across the clearing from the gorse tunnel. *Fireheart!*

I lengthened my stride and crashed into him, stretching out my front paws to run my claws down his flank. He shrieked and whirled to face me. Furious green eyes stared into mine, and he lunged toward me with his teeth bared. I knocked him away with a thrust of my head, then sank my claws into his ear and felt the thin flesh tear satisfyingly. Fireheart fell sideways, leaving his pale orange belly open to the sky. One slice with my claws and Tigerclaw would have to make good on his promise. . . .

Pain shot through my tail and I let out a screech. Whipping around, I saw a golden brown tom clinging to the tip with his teeth. He looked younger than the other warriors by several moons, his fur still kit-soft around his face, but the determination in his eyes made me flinch. I tried to back away but he didn't let go, and the agony in my tail made my eyes close for a moment. Behind me, I heard Fireheart scramble to his paws, out of reach. I couldn't fight them both. I clawed myself across the clearing, heading for the gorse. The young cat kept his jaws locked around my tail until I felt the bone splinter. With a final desperate haul, I made it to the tunnel. The cat released his grip and sprang away. Dazed with pain, I crawled into the gorse and fled, dragging my bleeding tail behind me.

Tigerclaw lost the battle. I made it back to the Twolegplace, where I hid behind a pile of stinking waste for two days, terrified that ThunderClan warriors would hunt me down, too scared to venture out for food or water. Finally, one of the exiled ShadowClan cats found me and saved my life by bringing me a scrawny bird that he'd found dead by the side of a Thunderpath. He said that warriors from the other side of the river came and helped drive out the invading cats. Tigerclaw had been forced out of the Clan a day later, and vanished. The ShadowClan cat sounded disappointed that Tigerclaw hadn't come looking for him again.

I told myself that it would be better to stay away from the Clan cats, to lead my own life without fear of having my tail bitten off or my eyes scratched out. But I couldn't forget the courage of the ThunderClan warriors as they united against us, the looks in their eyes as they turned their skills in pouncing and killing prey to protect their Clanmates and their home. I wanted to be a part of that, to know that other cats cared about what happened to me—and would spill their own blood for my sake. That awful, screeching battle had shown the best in these cats. And they were better than I could ever be.

When Tigerclaw came to the Twolegplace again, this time looking for cats to help him take over ShadowClan, I went with him. I don't know if he remembered me from the first battle, but he let me join his group of rogues, and together we proved our strength to ShadowClan until they let us become their Clanmates, and raised no argument when Tigerclaw announced that he would be their leader. I had found my place at last, and I will never regret the path that led me there. I took a warrior name, Nightwhisper.

Though my paws are stained with blood, and I once tried to kill the cat you know as Firestar, I would do it all again to live in the Clans. There is no life better than being a warrior, and no better way to prove your loyalty or your courage than in battle.

Graystripe Speaks: The Battle Against the Foxes

Really, you'd like to hear about the foxes? Great StarClan, that was moons ago, when we still lived in the forest! Firestar and Sandstorm had left the territory for a while, so as ThunderClan's deputy, I was leading the Clan. I had good warriors helping me, but there were whispers of trouble. A pack of foxes had made their dens beneath the roots of the Great Oak at Fourtrees, our normal Gathering site. To make matters worse, the foxes were stealing our prey. Usually foxes lived on their own, or with a pawful of skittish cubs, but these foxes seemed to have their own Clan, with patrols to keep us out and make raids for food.

Things came to a head at a Gathering like this, under a cold full moon early in leaf-bare. We were forced to meet that night at Snakerocks on ThunderClan's territory, not far from Fourtrees, but far enough inside our borders to make all the Clans nervous. All four Clans needed to deal with the foxes, and I had an idea. . . .

"Cats of all the Clans," I announced, feeling the stone of Snakerocks ice-cold and slippery beneath my paws. "I believe we can drive out the foxes if we work together."

"Since when did deputies take over the Gathering?" muttered a voice below me. It was Tornear of WindClan.

Blackstar stood up, his white coat glowing in the moonlight. "Graystripe speaks for ThunderClan while Firestar is . . . away."

I knew the ShadowClan leader was trying to find out where Firestar and Sandstorm had gone; I couldn't tell him because I didn't know, but I trusted Firestar when he told me that they would return, and in the meantime, I wasn't going to let any of the other Clans suspect that I had no idea where my leader was.

"We all know that foxes are most aggressive in their dens, when they are protecting their cubs," I began. My voice sounded as feeble as a kit's squeak on the still night air. "They are more vulnerable when they are hunting and their attention is fixed on something else. We should strike then, and show them that the forest belongs to us and us alone."

"You're suggesting a battle against foxes?" sneered a cat from the back of the crowd. I peered into the shadows but couldn't see who was speaking. "We'll be eaten alive!"

There were murmurs of agreement, and for a moment I felt a flash of anger. Were these cats willing to lie around and do nothing while foxes stole our prey and drove us out of the place where our ancestors had gathered for countless full moons?

"I'm not saying we should confront them in a regular battle. We will use each Clan's strengths to teach them a lesson," I pressed on. "We have the advantage of more training, more skills, more knowledge of the forest than these intruders."

I could see nods of interest, and a couple of my Clanmates called out encouragingly. There was no turning back now. I was about to lead all the Clans into a battle for survival in our own homes.

"I've picked up a scent!" Cloudtail hissed. His thick white fur stood out like a splash of snow against the withered bracken, but his difficulty in hiding had made his nose keener than most of his Clanmates'. The wind rattled the brown stalks around us, filling my ears with whispers, but at least it would hide our noise from our prey as well.

For once, this patrol wasn't in search of fresh-kill. Instead, we were hunting foxes. Above our heads, the gray sky was darkening with nightfall, and the air was filled with the echoing calls from a pair of owls. This was the time when the foxes went looking for food to steal; tonight they were about to find out that they had become the hunted!

Keeping his head low and his tail straight up, Cloudtail followed the scent trail along the bank of the stream at the top of ThunderClan's territory. I followed, with Mousefur, her apprentice, Spiderpaw, and Brightheart treading softly behind me. So far the trail had led toward the river, but I knew the foxes were no fonder of getting their paws wet than we were, so I wasn't surprised when Brightheart picked up the scent on the far side of the border, in the stretch of RiverClan territory that led from the bridge by the gorge to Fourtrees. The ground here was covered with rocks and scrubby bushes rather than trees, a good place for rabbits and low-roosting birds. I let out a sigh of relief. I had hoped the foxes would come here to hunt; that meant the other Clans were in the right place. I was beginning to realize how much of my plan depended on the foxes doing what I wanted them to.

A rustle up ahead warned us that we were nearly on their tails. Soon, a flash of glossy red fur behind a hawthorn thicket revealed our targets.

"Mousefur, have you got the rabbit?"

The dusky brown warrior padded forward, carrying a young rabbit, still warm and blood-scented.

"Away you go," I ordered.

Mousefur skirted the hawthorn thicket and let the rabbit's hind legs drop to the ground. As she walked away, the limp bundle of brown-and-white fluff left a pathetic trail in the dust, and the air quivered with the scent of the kill. I led the rest of the patrol in step with Mousefur, under cover of some bushes. *Foxes, foxes,* I called silently. *Can you smell this tasty meal?*

The branches of the hawthorn thicket crackled as if something large were turning around underneath. I held my breath. Would the foxes take the bait? I was using a trick I had learned from Tigerstar, when he lured the pack of dogs right into the ravine by laying a trail of dead rabbits. Brindleface had died in their attack; Mousefur was risking her life now, not just for ThunderClan but for every Clan in the forest. I had volunteered to carry the rabbit first, but Mousefur had insisted. She was faster than me, she said, adding that she had no qualms about dropping the rabbit and running for her life if the foxes got too close.

The softest crunch of sand told me that the foxes had picked up the scent trail and were beginning to stalk Mousefur. I hoped they were too dumb to wonder why a dead rabbit would be moving. I signaled with my tail to Mousefur, who was watching me with one eye, and she started to walk faster, keeping the rabbit dragging on the ground. The paw steps behind her sped up. Mousefur curved away from the ThunderClan border, heading for a copse of trees on the WindClan border. The foxes followed, and I had to break into a run to keep pace with them.

The trees loomed nearer above the scratchy bushes. *Come on! Where are you?* I thought desperately. Closer and closer... Mousefur wouldn't be able to carry the rabbit for much longer! Or the foxes might catch up to her...

"ShadowClan! Attack!" The still air was split with the sound of cats crashing out of the trees, led by Blackstar. I halted behind a lichen-covered rock with the rest of the patrol; a moment later, Mousefur joined us, panting and with her eyes shining.

"Perfect so far!" she declared.

Now it was time to let ShadowClan do what they did best: an ambush. We listened to them hurtling and shrieking through the bushes; there was a volley of startled yelps, then the sound of heavier animals plunging away, scrabbling over rocks. Just as I'd hoped, the ShadowClan ambush had frightened the foxes toward the river, where another surprise awaited them.

Once Mousefur had caught her breath, I raced out of the cover of the rock and followed the noise of the foxes and the ShadowClan cats. I burst out of the long grass that grew on the bank just as a line of RiverClan warriors splashed out of the water to meet the foxes. The RiverClan deputy, Mistyfoot, was at the head of the patrol, looking fierce with her fur slicked darkly against her back and her ears flattened.

The foxes—there were four of them, all full-grown—skidded to a halt and scrambled to turn tail, almost losing their footing on the slippery pebbles. Beyond them, I could hear ShadowClan plunging into the reeds, leaving a route clear back to Fourtrees.

"Come on," I yowled over my shoulder, and my Clanmates leaped beside me as I jumped down to the shore and raced to join the RiverClan warriors as they set off after the foxes. With a deafening clatter of reeds, the ShadowClan patrol emerged and we charged in a screeching line through the trail of broken undergrowth and overturned boulders left by our prey.

A false scent-trail and two ambushes, just to chase the foxes back to their own territory? I can see you're looking puzzled, little kittypets, but it was all part of my plan. We had to keep the foxes away from Fourtrees, and tire them out as much as possible, while the fourth battle patrol, from WindClan, took charge of the dens. Tallstar had agreed to send his best tunnelers, the cats who moved across the moor underground and were as comfortable in darkness as I was in sunlight, to flush out the cubs and trap them in the center of the clearing, where we had once held our Gatherings.

As the tops of the giant oaks appeared above the rim of the

hollow, an anguished yowl told me that the foxes had realized they'd been outwitted. I found an extra burst of speed in my paws, and skidded to a halt at the top of the slope. Below me, a ring of furious cats encircled a bundle of terrified baby foxes, keeping their backs to the cubs as they snarled at the approaching adults. There were cats from all four Clans in the battle line; I felt a flash of pride as I saw my Clanmates Dustpelt and Brackenfur take a step forward, daring the foxes to come any closer.

The rest of us made our way to the foot of the slope and watched in satisfaction as the foxes spun around and snarled when they saw they were trapped. There was still a danger they would try to fight us, but I was relying on the foxes being too afraid for the safety of their young to tackle both lines of cats. The biggest fox, a male with patches of darker red on his fur, took a pace toward us, baring his yellow teeth. Beside me, Spiderpaw let out a tiny whimper. I rested my tail on his flank, trying to give him courage.

Blackstar padded forward. "Leave our forest, and your cubs will be left alone," he ordered.

The fox blinked, and I guessed he couldn't understand us any more than we knew what they were saying with their ugly yelps and barks. But Blackstar's message was clear, even without the exact words.

"Yes, leave!" I joined in, arching my back and spitting. All along the foot of the slope, the patrols snarled at the foxes, making even the leader flinch. He glanced over his shoulder and saw the line of cats surrounding his precious cubs, each one with his or her claws unsheathed, ready to fight. He tossed his head as if he were shaking water from his fur, then barked. The foxes beside him lowered their heads and crouched down until their tails brushed the ground.

I stared in disbelief. The foxes were surrendering! We had won!

I was about to let out a yowl of joy when Mudclaw, the WindClan deputy, called from the line: "Fourtrees patrol! Stand aside!"

The line of cats split and moved to each side of the hollow. At once the cubs raced over to their parents, whimpering and snapping. The adult foxes swept them close with their tails, then turned to face us. The male fox snarled and flattened his ears, but he knew as well as we did that they had no option. The Clans had proven that the forest belonged to us. With one final growl, the leader of the foxes trotted up the slope with his pack behind him, the cubs stumbling to keep up. For a moment the foxes were silhouetted against the sky at the top of the hollow; then they vanished over the edge.

Blackstar turned to me. "Congratulations, Graystripe. Firestar would be very proud of you."

Then the other cats crowded around me, cheering and yowling our triumph to the first glowing stars. I stood with my paws rooted to the ground and bathed in the feeling of success. All four Clans had united behind me, and I had led them to victory. The battle against the foxes had been won, and Fourtrees was ours once more!

"THE BATTLE AGAINST THE FOXES"

PART FOUR: IN THE MIDST OF BATTLE

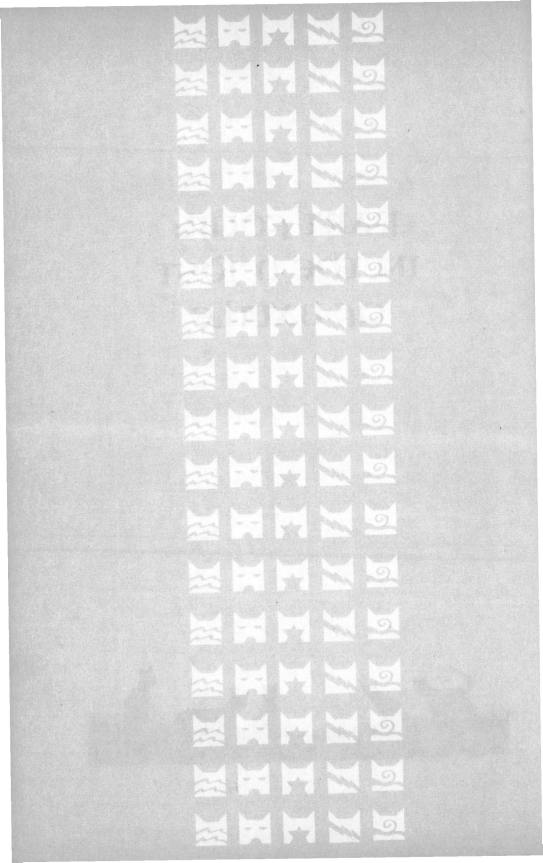

A LONG TRADITION

✻

The elders are talkative tonight! Oh, sorry, Graystripe, I didn't see you there. Greetings, kittypets. Welcome to the island. My name is Mistystar, the leader of RiverClan. Onestar told me that you've come to hear about our long tradition of battles. Well, you're in the right place for the best stories. But I hope you've seen that there's more to the Clans than fighting. Warriors train for a long time before they are allowed to risk spilling their own blood for their Clanmates.

Being in the thick of a battle can be a whirl of excitement and triumph. Still, there's always a dazzling fear, and the screeching and thud of bodies around you stay in your mind for moons. There are moments of ice-cold clarity, too, such as the sight of a fleeing enemy,

the satisfaction of a well-aimed blow, the sting of an injury when you don't dodge fast enough, or the heart-dropping cry of "Retreat!"

Every apprentice longs to fight, and every warrior remembers his first battle. For the ones who have trained hard enough and keep their heads in the maelstrom, it won't be their last.

Every warrior has a story to tell about memorable clashes. Just don't let them whet your appetite too much. Whitewing will share her first battle with you—the white she-cat over there with the ThunderClan warriors, see her? And Mousefur can tell you about a warrior named Lionheart who walks with StarClan now, but who would not mind you hearing about the time he lacked courage—and learned from it. Then, if there is time before dawn, you should listen to Cedarheart of ShadowClan. He has the longest memory of all the warriors, and he'll tell you about a ThunderClan leader who lived many, many moons ago, and his struggle for peace.

<hr/>

Whitewing Speaks: My First Battle

The first time I fought wasn't in a skirmish over some cats stepping over the ThunderClan border, or a piece of stolen prey. The enemies in the battle weren't even cats: They were badgers. Huge, fierce creatures with shadows streaking their fur and burning eyes; the snap of thorn-sharp teeth still echoes in my dreams, with the shrieks of my Clanmates as they are battered by a foe with no code of honor, no respect for our courage or skills. They came seeking vengeance because we had driven out a female and her cubs when we arrived at the lake. But they didn't want territory or fresh-kill. They wanted our blood.

I saw them first. I was returning to the hollow with my mentor, Brackenfur, after a training session. I was bouncing on air, proud that I'd finally mastered the leap-and-hold. Brackenfur must have been aching from the number of times he'd let me scramble onto his back and attempt to hold him down. Tufts of his fur clogged my claws; I was looking forward to cleaning them while I told my mother, Brightheart, about my new battle skill. The sun was sinking into the lake behind us as we approached the camp. Brackenfur's pelt glowed pink and gold in the slanting rays. My belly growled, and I thought hungrily of fresh-kill.

There was a crackle in the bracken at the end of the abandoned Thunderpath, and I looked over, expecting to see one of my Clanmates emerging. Beside me, Brackenfur stopped.

"Whitepaw, go inside the camp," he ordered.

I put my head to one side and looked up at him. "Why? What's wrong?"

"Just go!" he snapped. His fur was standing on end and his nostrils flared. Had he scented something?

I opened my mouth and took a deep breath. A sour smell hit the back of my throat. *Yuck!* I started to ask Brackenfur what it was when the bracken rustled and a long, thin snout poked out. It was black with a broad white stripe, and a bead of moisture hung at the end, as if whatever it belonged to was slavering with anticipation.

There was a rumble of thunder from the trees—no, not thunder—*roaring*, a low, angry bellow that got steadily louder. The muzzle in the bracken opened and a snarl came out.

"Get inside now!" Brackenfur spat, and I ran. I burst through the thorns with my ears flat back, trying to block out the noise that filled the forest, bounced around the walls of the hollow, swept over me like a wave coming nearer and nearer. . . .

Brackenfur pounded beside me, panting with fear. We stumbled into the center of the camp and Squirrelflight was leaping to her paws, her eyes growing wide in horror as the barrier crashed down behind us.

"Badger!" she yowled.

The clearing exploded with cats. I spotted my mother, Brightheart, pelting across the clearing to me, her good eye stretched so wide that it seemed almost white.

She shook her head. "Come with me. I've got to get Daisy and her kits out of the camp. You can hide with them at the top of the cliff."

I planted my paws more firmly on the grass. "No! I want to stay and fight!"

"Don't be a mouse-brain," snapped Brightheart. "This is no place for an apprentice. I want you where I know you'll be safe."

I looked up to the top of the hollow, which was circled with dense bushes. "There might be badgers up there, too," I pointed out.

"You'll be in the thickest patch of thorns I can find!" my mother hissed. "Stop arguing and follow me!"

"I want to fight!" I wailed.

There was a flash of white and Cloudtail appeared beside me. "What's going on?"

"Whitepaw needs to leave the camp with Daisy and her kits," Brightheart told him.

"But I want to stay!" I scowled.

"There isn't time for this!" Brightheart spat. "Have you seen what's happening?" She flicked her tail around the clearing, and I looked past her at a whirling storm of fur and teeth and claws. Spiderleg and Sootfur were attacking a female badger from both sides, springing forward to land a claws-out blow on her ears before leaping out of the way as she swung her massive head toward them.

I turned back to my mother. "Let me fight," I begged. "My Clanmates need me."

"She's right," Cloudtail put in unexpectedly. "This is what she has trained for. We need all the warriors we can get right now."

"She's not a warrior!" Brightheart hissed, and in her eyes I saw her fear that I was too young, too small, too inexperienced.

"If I survive this, I will be," I meowed softly.

My mother looked at me, then nodded. "Don't let her out of your sight, Cloudtail," she ordered without taking her gaze from me. Then she spun around and raced for the nursery, where Squirrelflight was standing guard.

Cloudtail opened his mouth to speak, but a huge shadow fell

across him and he looked up, shutting his jaws with a snap. A badger loomed over us, fury gleaming in its tiny black eyes. With a roar, it struck out with one front paw and sent Cloudtail spinning across the clearing. I backed away, desperately trying to think of the battle moves I'd just learned. But I was aware only of the ground under my paws and the tip of my tail brushing against brambles. I thought how pale I must look against the dark green thorns, my white pelt shining like the full moon. *I'm over here! Come and eat me!*

The badger opened its jaws, revealing pointed yellow teeth and a lolling red tongue. I wondered if it would hurt much when the badger sank its teeth into me. Everything seemed to have gone quiet; had the rest of the fighting stopped?

"Leave her alone!" There was a screech somewhere behind the badger, and a heavy white shape launched itself onto the creature's shoulders. Cloudtail! The badger reared backward and snaked its neck around, trying to bite him.

The noise of the battle crashed into my ears, and the ground beneath me trembled as bodies thudded around the hollow. I unsheathed my claws and sprang up, reaching for the badger's tiny curled ears. The pelt was thinnest there, just like on a cat, so I stood the best chance of reaching skin. I thumped against the side of the badger's head and tried to catch hold, but my paws slipped off the stinking black fur. Looking down, I realized in horror that my claws were so filled with hair from Brackenfur's pelt after our training session that I couldn't sink them into the badger's flesh.

I fell back to the ground with a thud and frantically yanked the fur out with my teeth. I rolled sideways, between the badger's front and hind legs. Then sensing a pointed muzzle swooping down toward me, I leaped for its ear again, and this time my claws ripped into soft skin. I clung on, scrabbling with my hind legs against the badger's shoulder.

Cloudtail was on the other side of the creature, staring up at me in amazement.

"Go help Brightheart!" I screeched. "You have to get Daisy's kits out!"

To my relief, he whipped around and vanished into the throng of cats. Badgers reared among them like black-and-white islands looming over a swirling brown-and-tabby lake. Beneath me, my badger bucked and plunged downward, trying to flip me off. I wrenched my claws free from its ear, wincing as an arc of blood spattered across my eyes, and sprang away just as the badger crashed onto the ground.

I had never felt more alive. On the far side of the hollow, Squirrelflight led Daisy up the tiny path to the top of the cliff. Brightheart, Cloudtail, and Brambleclaw followed, each carrying one of Daisy's kits. *StarClan, please let them be safe*, I prayed.

"Whitepaw!" There was a wail from the bottom of the cliff,

and I saw my denmate Birchpaw crouching with his back to the stone as a male badger padded toward him. The badger moved slowly, knowing his prey was trapped.

"Climb, Birchpaw!" I yowled. His eyes met mine, huge and dark with terror, and for a moment I thought he had frozen to the spot, but then he turned and began scrabbling at the rock with his front paws.

"Reach higher!" I called, spotting a paw hold a mouse-length above his head. Birchpaw pushed with his hind feet and sank his claws into the dirt lodged in a crevice in the cliff. He hauled himself up, his haunches dangling behind him, and hung from one paw.

"Come on! Climb higher!" I hissed through my teeth, knowing he wouldn't be able to hear me now.

Miraculously, Birchpaw found a place to grip with his hind paws and started to heave himself farther up the wall. But then his front leg twisted and his claws slid out of the crevice, and I watched in horror as my denmate slithered down, down, down, to where the badger waited for him with one paw raised for a killing blow.

"Birchpaw!" I screamed, and shut my eyes, waiting for the final strike.

There was a roar from the badger—not of triumph but of rage. I opened my eyes and saw the creature hunched over a crack at the foot of the cliff. There was a flash of light brown fur against the stone, and I realized that Birchpaw had somehow squeezed himself out of reach. Until the badger's fury tore apart the stone and it launched itself on Birchpaw . . .

In three bounds, I reached the badger and crouched down by its haunches. *Leap-and-hold.* That was the only way I could inflict any real damage. *Jump now, while it's distracted.*

"Help!" Birchpaw yowled from his tiny hiding place.

I pressed down with my hind paws and sprang onto the

badger, landing with my paws on either side of its spine. I thrust my claws through the dense, bristly fur and kept my weight low as the creature reared up, twisting as it tried to bite me. I wasn't here just to hang on; I needed to injure it enough to get it away from Birchpaw. Sinking in deeper with my hind claws, I released one front paw and slashed at the badger's face as it turned toward me. My foot shot through the air and I nearly lost my balance. Clinging on, I tried again, and this time felt a satisfying wrench in my front leg as I made contact with the badger's cheek and ripped a long wound from the corner of its eye to its jaw.

The creature bellowed in pain and hauled itself away from the foot of the cliff. I saw Birchpaw scramble out. He left a thick trail of blood and his face was swollen, but he was alive. His mother, Ferncloud, raced over to him and sheltered him with her body as they fled around the edge of the hollow.

I clung on to the badger as it plunged and snapped. *You tried to kill my friend!* I had saved Birchpaw's life, but there was no time to savor the victory. I sliced again and again with my claws, scoring deep wounds through the badger's pelt until my paws were tufted with black-and-white fur. The creature started to sink to its knees and I braced myself, ready to jump free when it tried to roll over and crush me. The badger's muzzle thudded onto the ground and it let out a long groan as it slumped onto its belly. I stayed crouched on its back, wondering if this was a new trick.

"Whitepaw, get off!" It was Dustpelt, yowling to me from halfway up a hawthorn bush. "You've won!"

Dazed, I sprang down to the ground and stared at my enemy. Its eyes were half-closed, and its breath came in quick, shallow gasps. Had I really killed a badger?

Teeth sank into the scruff of my neck and I let out a yelp of fear.

"Get away from it! It's not dead!" Dustpelt hissed in my ear as he dragged me away. "But you did well to stun it. Come on, stay close."

He led me to the hawthorn tree and shoved me into the branches. I clung to a swaying twig, catching my breath and gazing out at the hollow. The stone walls were streaked with blood, and the grass was hidden beneath writhing bodies—and ominous furry lumps where cats had fallen and not gotten up again. My legs ached from the effort of holding on to the badger, and my eyes stung from the rancid blood, but I couldn't stay here. My Clanmates needed me.

I scrambled down the tree and ran out into the clearing. A badger with one ear almost completely torn off lunged toward me; wondering briefly whether that was the badger that had attacked Cloudtail and me at the start, I swerved away and fled toward the barrier—or what remained of the barrier, after the badgers had trampled it down. A shadow fell across me, and I looked up at a narrow black-and-white face. I tried to dodge away, but one of my paws was trapped under a bramble. I flattened myself to the ground and let out a wail.

"StarClan, help me!"

Paws thudded toward me, and Squirrelflight sprang to my side, front paws raised. I waited for her to strike, but there was a pause. Peering up, I saw the she-cat staring in astonishment at the badger that was about to eat me. In a strange, high-pitched voice, she meowed, "It's okay, Whitepaw. This is Midnight."

The badger that had told the Clans where to find their new home when they were driven out of the old forest had come to help us—bringing warriors from WindClan, fresh and hungry for victory. They fought alongside my Clanmates and drove out the badgers, giving them scars to remember us by. We had won the battle—but at a terrible cost. Rainwhisker, Sootfur, and Cinderpelt all died in the attack.

Every ThunderClan cat was a hero that day. Sometimes I think my pelt still smells of blood, and when I'm hunting alone in the woods, every rustle reminds me of badgers marching against my home. We were saved by our battle skills, and we will use them again if we must.

Mousefur Speaks: The Deserter

This story takes place in the old forest, on the border beside the Thunderpath. Our territory ended here, and ShadowClan's began on the other side. Lionpaw was on a border patrol with his mentor, Swiftbreeze, his denmate Bluepaw, and her mentor, Sunfall, the ThunderClan deputy. The scent of ShadowClan was too strong to be drifting across the Thunderpath on the wind—there was barely a breeze on this cold, gray day in early newleaf.

Sunfall had led his patrol close to the edge of the Thunderpath, carefully sniffing each bush for signs of trespassers.

"Well, look what we have here!" came a snarl from the foot of a beech tree. "A patrol of ThunderClan warriors! Ooh, I'm scared now!"

A bright ginger tom stepped forward, still curling his lip, and blocked their way.

Sunfall halted and allowed the fur to rise on his neck. "You're trespassing, Foxheart," he growled. "What are you doing on this side of the Thunderpath?"

Foxheart looked back at his Clanmates. "Great StarClan, these warriors ask difficult questions! What are we doing here, Crowtail?"

A skinny black she-cat put her head to one side, pretending to think. Then she straightened up. "I remember! We're *hunting prey.*"

Lionpaw gulped. There was something in the way the she-cat had looked straight at him that made him feel as if her prey were ThunderClan apprentices. He glanced at Swiftbreeze, but she was glaring at the intruders, her tail kinked stiffly over her back.

A small white tom, his face still fringed with fluffy kit fur, padded forward to stand beside Crowtail. "We're chasing a rabbit," he announced. "It came from our territory, which means it's still ours."

"That's enough, Cloudpaw." A flash of anger swept across Foxheart's expression, and Lionpaw wondered whether the apprentice would get in trouble later on for speaking up. "We don't have to explain ourselves."

Another cat emerged, his dark gray pelt well hidden among the shadows beneath the tree. "That's right. ThunderClan patrols don't scare us."

"Well, they should!" Bluepaw hissed, unsheathing her claws. "We're not afraid of you!"

Lionpaw looked sideways at his denmate. *Really? You're not scared?* He looked back at the ShadowClan cats, all of them so much bigger than he was, with long, curved claws and powerful shoulders. And a hunger in their eyes that yearned for more than fresh-kill.

Sunfall lifted his head. "Leave now, and this matter will be forgotten."

"Or what?" Foxheart asked with a hint of a growl.

"Or we'll make you leave," snarled Swiftbreeze, taking one step forward.

Foxheart let out a hiss. "Oh, I'm going to enjoy this," he murmured. His gaze fell on Lionpaw. "I'll start with that trembling lump of fur over there. I'll slice his ears so he can't hear his own screams of pain, then shred his muzzle until he begs to be put out of his agony."

Sunfall let out a yowl and sprang toward the ShadowClan cat. Swiftbreeze leaped forward beside him, and Bluepaw crouched down with her claws out. Lionpaw's vision blurred and the blood roared in his ears. He couldn't fight these cats! *StarClan, save me!*

He spun around on numb, shaking paws and scrabbled across the damp forest floor. All he could think of was getting far, far away from those terrible cats.

Suddenly a log reared up in front of him and he crashed into the furrowed gray bark. Reeling back, he sat down hard, dazed and bruised. Where did he think he was running to? He couldn't leave the territory: Where would he go? How would he survive? But he couldn't go back to the camp. His Clanmates would know he had been too scared to fight ShadowClan warriors. He might not even be allowed to go back. Pinestar might send him away! Warriors were supposed to have courage in the face of the fiercest enemies, but Lionpaw had none. Icy drops of rain started to fall, bouncing on his fur and making him shiver. Looking around, he realized that he had run all the way to Snakerocks, the pile of rugged gray stones in the middle of the forest where adders lived. Only in hot weather, though—in leaf-bare, the snakes hid themselves away, leaving the rocks safe for hunting. And shelter. Lionpaw spotted a shadowed entrance at the foot of the stones and trotted over to it. The cave stretched farther back than he could see, and smelled of fox, but the scent was old and stale, and Lionpaw couldn't hear anything moving about inside. He could stay here for a while, maybe catch something to eat, and figure out what he was going to do next. He squeezed through the gap and lay down on the bare earth, pressing his back against the rock. It was cold and uncomfortable compared with his mossy nest in the apprentices' den, but he didn't let himself think about that. He'd have to get used to finding other places to shelter, now that he couldn't be a Clan cat.

He didn't mean to sleep, but when he looked out of the entrance again the forest was hidden in shadow, and a few stars twinkled in the branches. Lionpaw looked at his paws, feeling his fur burn with shame. Were his warrior ancestors gazing down at him with anger that he had run away from the battle? Or shame that he had failed his Clanmates and broken the warrior code? Or pity that he was such a pathetic, useless apprentice that he couldn't stand his ground against a few trespassers?

There was a rustle on the far side of the clearing. Lionpaw stiffened, bristling. Had the ShadowClan cats tracked him down to make good on their threats? Or was a hungry fox looking for a meal? Lionpaw started to back into the cave, one paw at a time.

"Lionpaw, are you there?"

"I definitely caught his scent back there, but it's harder out in

"THE VICTORIOUS CLAN"

the open," complained another voice.

"Keep trying. Please, StarClan, don't let him have left the territory."

Lionpaw blinked. Swiftbreeze and Bluepaw were looking for him! He shrank farther back beneath the rock. Were they going to punish him for running away? Then his lip curled in disgust. *What are you doing, cowering from your own Clanmates? You may have been too much of a coward to face ShadowClan, but you can stand up and take your punishment!*

Trying not to whimper with shame, he crept out of the cave. Two shapes were just visible in the darkness.

"Swiftbreeze! I've picked up his trail!" Bluepaw mewed excitedly.

"I'm here," Lionpaw croaked.

There was the sound of paw steps; then Swiftbreeze and Bluepaw were curling around him, pressing their warm pelts against his flanks and purring louder than a horde of bees.

"Oh, thank StarClan we found you!" Swiftbreeze murmured. "You silly mouse-brain, we've been worried!"

"You missed a good old skirmish, too!" Bluepaw chirped. "Adderfang and Thistlepaw showed up just in time to give those ShadowClan warriors a bashing they won't forget! I can't believe they thought we'd let them hunt on our territory!"

Lionpaw pulled himself away and hung his head. "I'm sorry I ran away," he blurted out. "Have you come to punish me?"

Swiftbreeze paused, and he could tell she was looking at him through the half-light. "Punish you?"

"Yes, for being scared!"

There was a rustle of movement, and Lionpaw felt his mentor lick his ear. "Oh, Lionpaw, every cat gets scared sometimes. Even the strongest warriors."

"Yeah, even I got a bit scared today!" Bluepaw added.

Swiftbreeze's breath was warm on Lionpaw's ear. "You shouldn't have run away. You should have trusted your Clanmates to protect you—do you really think I'd let any cat hurt you? I'd be a pretty useless mentor if I sent my apprentice into battle before I'd taught him how to take care of himself!"

"But what if I'm always too scared to fight?" Lionpaw asked in a small voice. "I can't be a warrior like that."

Swiftbreeze purred. "If you don't feel any fear, you will never be able to feel brave. Courage is nothing without the knowledge of what you face. Give me time to teach you how to fight and defend yourself, and use the size and weight of your enemy against him. Then you'll find courage deep inside."

She moved away, and Lionpaw felt the air chill against his flank. "Now, come back to the camp," she meowed more briskly. "I bet you haven't had anything to eat all day. Pinestar wants to speak with you"—Lionpaw swallowed hard—"but he won't punish you. You'll be a great warrior one day, I promise."

She started to walk back across the clearing, and Lionpaw ran to catch up. His heart swelled with relief and love for his Clanmates. Maybe Swiftbreeze was right: Because he had known what it was like to be really, really scared, he would understand more about courage. And when he had an apprentice, he would teach them that it was okay to be frightened sometimes. In fact, it was a sign of the best warriors!

Cedarheart Speaks:
The Leader Who Sought Peace

It began at a Gathering, not here on the island but in the hollow with the four Great Oak trees, back in the forest. The ThunderClan leader, Morningstar, stood on the Great Rock beneath the shadows of the oak trees and let his voice cut through the icy air. "If all five Clans are here, let the Gathering begin!"

There were murmurs and shuffles from below as the cats found places to sit among their Clanmates, and scowled at other Clans who dared to push too close. Morningstar waited impatiently, feeling his paws freeze to the stone. Behind him, the other leaders shifted their haunches; the rock was painfully cold to sit on, but only one leader at a time stood to address the Clans.

"Cats of all Clans, WindClan is stealing our prey!" Morningstar announced.

"What? How dare you accuse us?" snarled a cat below him; the WindClan leader, Rabbitstar, let out a hiss from the back of the rock.

Morningstar let his gaze fall across all the Clans. "I don't want WindClan to try to deny it," he went on. "They know it's true; we've seen their warriors too many times inside our borders, chasing voles and mice instead of rabbits. I'm not challenging them to a battle, either."

A ripple of surprise rose from the WindClan cats.

"I'm not scared of fighting them!" yowled a ThunderClan warrior.

Morningstar sighed. "I know you're not, Beechfur. But we are in no position to challenge them. Our Clan is weaker than we have ever been, weaker than we should be even in the middle of leaf-bare."

Wails of protest came from his Clan. "No, Morningstar! You can't say that!"

"Do you want every Clan in the forest to help themselves?"

"Why are you doing this?"

Morningstar pushed on. "We've had too many kits born recently, and our elders have started to refuse food for the sake of the queens. We're surviving on crow-food found by the side of the Thunderpath because we're too weak to hunt fresh-kill."

"Morningstar, stop! You're destroying us!" snarled his deputy, Leafstorm, who was at the foot of the rock. From the shadow cast by moonlight, he could tell she was standing up on her hind legs, craning to see him on top.

"I don't want my Clan to fight," Morningstar meowed. "Instead, we should share what prey there is among all the Clans, and help one another through leaf-bare until our hunting grounds are full again. If we join together as one, we will all survive."

Willowstar, the RiverClan leader, sprang to her paws. "Why should I care if ThunderClan is starving? My loyalty is to my own cats! You are a fool if you thought we'd agree to this, Morningstar.

RiverClan keeps its own prey!"

Rabbitstar jumped up. "My cats wouldn't eat your slimy fish anyway! We'd rather go hungry!"

Sedgestar of ShadowClan joined in more calmly. "My Clan is bigger than any of yours, so we can't spare any fresh-kill. We have enough to feed ourselves, and I won't let any of my cats go hungry for the sake of our rivals."

SkyClan's leader, Fennelstar, nodded. "Our warrior ancestors have given us territories according to our skills. It's up to us to survive on that legacy. Morningstar, you shame your ancestors if you cannot feed your Clan within your boundaries."

"Perhaps this is a test from StarClan?" Rabbitstar suggested. "There is too much weakness in the forest, and only the strongest Clans deserve to survive." He flashed a glance at Morningstar. "I'd say that my Clan was doing pretty well right now."

Morningstar shook his head. "I cannot believe that our ancestors would willingly let us starve to prove a point."

"You're letting yourselves starve if you can't protect your borders," Willowstar commented, with a hint of smugness.

Morningstar faced Rabbitstar again. "If you choose to keep stealing prey from my territory, you will be breaking the warrior code. My Clan is too weak to fight you. I'm asking for mercy until our prey starts running again."

"You're the weak one, old cat," sneered Rabbitstar. "Better start sniffing out that crow-food, because you won't be having any fresh-kill for a while."

Morningstar began to pick his way down the Great Rock. Normally he would jump down, but his legs were trembling with hunger. He couldn't remember the last meal he'd eaten. The elders weren't the only ThunderClan cats giving up their food for the nursing queens. "I have nothing more to say," he meowed over his shoulder. "Our fate is in your paws."

He wound through the cats, who parted like rippling grass to let him pass. His Clanmates waited for him at the foot of the slope, their eyes flashing with anger and their pelts bristling. Morningstar pushed past them and led them out of the hollow without giving them a chance to speak. Leafstorm caught up to him, panting.

"Are you out of your mind? You've just invited every other Clan to help themselves to our territory and our prey!" She was furious, and for a moment Morningstar saw her unsheathed claws gleam in the moonlight.

"We will not fight WindClan over this," he repeated. "Tomorrow I want you to take a patrol of warriors to Rabbitstar and speak to him again. We are too quick to use violence to solve everything. If we fight now, we'll lose half our Clan with the first strike. Can't you see I'm trying to protect us?"

Leafstorm glared at him, her green eyes hot. "All I see is a leader who's too scared to go into battle!"

Morningstar started to protest, but the ginger she-cat leaped ahead of him into the trees. Several warriors followed her, leaving Morningstar padding alone through the frost-dappled forest. A puffing sound behind him made him look back; Mothwhisker, an elder, was hobbling to catch up. Morningstar stopped to wait.

"Thanks," wheezed Mothwhisker. The two cats walked on slowly, their breath clouding around them. "You meant what you said back there, didn't you?" Mothwhisker rasped.

"Yes," Morningstar replied. "The Clan is too weak to fight right now."

He expected Mothwhisker to agree with him; elders knew better than most cats how fragile a hold warriors had on life, and how dangerous a battle would be on hollow bellies. But

Mothwhisker was shaking his head.

"You're wrong, Morningstar," he muttered. "Oh, we may be weak, but you should never have let WindClan know. They must be hungry, too, or they wouldn't be stealing our prey. We should strike them by surprise, take the battle right to their camp, and show them that ThunderClan borders are as strong as they ever were."

Morningstar stopped and rounded on the elderly tom. "I will not lead my Clan into a needless battle!" he spat. Memories filled his mind of a light brown tabby with amber eyes and white front paws, as if she had stepped up to her knees in snow. The last time he had seen her, she had been so drenched in her own blood that he couldn't see a fleck of white fur underneath. She had died curled protectively around her belly, which was just beginning to swell with her kits—his kits, too. Morningstar had never known which ShadowClan warrior struck the killing blow. Anyway, what good would vengeance do? It wouldn't bring her back.

"We lost Songbird in a battle that should never have been fought," he hissed. "We had no proof that ShadowClan chased that fox into our territory. Getting rid of it used up too much of our strength; I was stupid to let my pride send a patrol after ShadowClan as well."

"Leaders have to be proud of their Clans," Mothwhisker murmured. "Would you rather be ashamed of us? Tell every Clan that we're too feeble to defend our borders anymore?"

Morningstar started walking again. "I'm not ashamed of any cat," he growled. "You don't understand. I've made my decision, and that's the end of it."

Leafstorm returned the next day with a slash along her flank that the medicine cat, Pearnose, struggled to close. The warriors who had gone with her to WindClan bore their own wounds. The patrol had barely crossed the border when WindClan cats attacked them; Leafstorm suspected they'd been lying in wait.

"Of course, we couldn't fight them off," she spat, clenching her teeth as Pearnose pressed another pawful of cobweb against her injury. "They outnumbered us and were fat from feasting on our prey!"

"We didn't smell them before they attacked because they were covered in our own scent," added Pineclaw. One of his ears had been ripped right to the tip, and scarlet blood streaked his dark brown fur.

"We may as well let them live here and make their hunting easier," growled Featherwing. The pale gray she-cat had one eye swollen shut and claw marks sliced across her cheek.

"I'm sorry," Morningstar meowed. "Clearly WindClan is without honor." He turned to walk away down the tunnel of ferns that led to the clearing.

"They have no honor because they are *thieves*!" Leafstorm yowled after him. She broke into a coughing fit, gasping for breath.

Morningstar winced. Leafstorm had been coughing for days. He'd suggested she stay back from the Gathering, but she'd insisted on coming. He'd thought that meant she was feeling better. As he reached the clearing, Pearnose scampered along the tunnel and joined him. The brown tabby's eyes were serious.

"Morningstar, can we talk? In private, I mean."

"Sure." He led her to his den beneath Highrock. They pushed through the screen of lichen that hung across the entrance, and the medicine cat settled herself neatly on the sandy floor opposite Morningstar's nest.

"I think Leafstorm has greencough," she announced.

Morningstar stared at her in dismay. "But . . . but she went all the way to WindClan today! And fought!"

Pearnose narrowed her eyes. "She shouldn't have done either of those things; nor should she have gone to the Gathering last night. She's been sick for more than a moon, and I warned her it would get worse if she didn't rest. But she's been hunting every day, you know, often two or three times. And I haven't seen her take anything for herself since Mossheart's kits were born."

Morningstar let his shoulders slump. His Clan was dying around him, and he could do nothing to protect it.

Beechfur poked his head through the lichen. "Sorry to disturb you, Morningstar, but I wondered if you wanted me to lead a border patrol? Mossheart said Leafstorm was sick."

Morningstar lifted his head. "There will be no more border patrols," he ordered. "I want every warrior, every apprentice, to look for food. We'll all get sick if we don't have something to eat."

Beechfur's eyes were very round. "Wha . . . what? No border patrols at all? But . . . WindClan and SkyClan will take everything!"

"Not if we catch it first. You're wasting time! Go!" Morningstar dismissed the warrior with a flick of his tail. As the lichen quivered behind him, Morningstar turned back to Pearnose. He sighed. "Are you going to tell me that I'm doing the wrong thing as well?"

The medicine cat shook her head. "You know me better than that, Morningstar. I would not walk in your paws for all the mice in the forest. Your path is lonelier than I could bear. Now, I must go and send Fallowpaw to look for catmint at the edge of Twolegplace. If we're lucky, some will have survived the frost."

She slipped out of the den. Beyond the clearing, Leafstorm's coughs split the air. Morningstar heaved himself to his paws. He could hunt as well as any of his warriors. He'd find something for Leafstorm to eat, to get her strength back. He should have seen how thin she had become long before now. Battles or not, he needed his deputy beside him.

A quarter moon passed. It was getting hard to remember where the fresh-kill pile was supposed to be. Any prey that was caught, any scraps of crow-food, were eaten at once. Queens first, then warriors, then apprentices. Morningstar took charge of feeding Leafstorm. She tried to refuse, but he threatened to lean on her wound if she didn't eat. Now he stood staring at a lump of black feathers that might have been a bird once, but was so mangled and frozen that it could have been a piece of wood instead.

"Is this all you could find?" he demanded.

Pineclaw curled his lip. "No, actually. There are squirrels and mice all over the place out there, but I thought you'd prefer this."

Morningstar winced. "It's okay. I know you're doing your best."

"But WindClan is doing better!" Featherwing argued. "They don't even try to hide from us now! They just march in and stalk our prey as if we were nothing but unwelcome visitors."

"I went along the border this morning, looking for yarrow, and I couldn't even tell where our scent marks were supposed to be," put in Pearnose's apprentice, Fallowpaw.

"You gave WindClan a chance to have mercy," Beechfur meowed more gently. "They have shown us none. We should stop having mercy on them."

Morningstar gritted his teeth. *StarClan, why are you destroying my Clan? I only want peace for them!*

Suddenly, Pearnose burst into the clearing. "Leafstorm is dead!" she wailed.

Morningstar stared at her in disbelief. "No . . ." His brave, quarrelsome, sharp-minded deputy couldn't be *dead*. Not from a cough.

"She was too thin to fight the infection," Pearnose murmured, her breath warm on his ear.

"You mean I killed her," Morningstar rasped.

Pearnose drew back in horror. "No! You tried to feed her, but she was too sick. Please don't blame yourself."

"Leafstorm wanted to die in battle," whispered another voice beside him.

Morningstar spun around, his nostrils flaring as he breathed in the sweet, familiar scent. *Songbird?*

"At least I had that chance," the voice continued.

Morningstar narrowed his eyes and made out a faint outline of a brown tabby she-cat. He could see his warriors standing behind her; they were gazing at him with concern in their eyes, as if they didn't know what he had just seen.

"Songbird," he breathed.

"Let your warriors fight," she told him. "Let them prove their courage and their loyalty to you by defending your borders. Peace is not the way of the Clans. We prove ourselves in battle."

Her outline wavered like mist, and Morningstar bounded forward. "Songbird! Wait!"

He blinked, and the clearing was empty apart from his warriors and Pearnose, looking uncertainly at him. How could he have doubted their courage? Hunger wouldn't weaken their desire to win; instead, it would sharpen their claws, lend power to each strike. Leafstorm was dead because he had not fought to keep ThunderClan's prey safe from thieves. If any more cats were to die, it would be honorably, in battle, not starved like a helpless kit.

"Who will join me in battle against WindClan?" he roared.

There was a moment of shocked silence; then his warriors straightened up, lifting their heads and letting the fur bristle along their spines. "We will," they yowled.

More cats emerged from the dens around them, their eyes brighter than Morningstar had seen in a long time. "We're really going to fight?" one of them asked.

"We are," vowed Morningstar. He turned to Pearnose. "Prepare your supplies. Fallowpaw will help you." His gaze fell on a patchy gray-and-brown pelt among the throng of cats. "So will Mothwhisker. I know he wants to serve his Clan once more." His eyes met the elder's, and they nodded to each other.

Then Morningstar lifted his tail and faced the gorse tunnel that led out of the camp.

"ThunderClan, attack!"

PART FIVE:
THE AFTERMATH

CEDARHEART'S
FINAL WARNING

❅

So, young kittypets, you have walked in the memories of our finest warriors, shared in the thrill of the fight, felt teeth meet in your fur, and struck out with your paws to bruise your enemy before they can deal a killing blow. Has your curiosity been satisfied? There is one more lesson to learn about battles: that the echoes last long after the final blow has been struck and every wound has healed. With each challenge and each blow landed, lives are changed forever.

Before I take you back to Onestar, there is a story to tell from long ago, when there were still five Clans in the forest. ThunderClan and SkyClan argued for many moons over the land on their shared border. So much blood was spilled that Darkstar, the leader of SkyClan, decided to give it to ThunderClan at a Gathering. His Clanmates were horrified, especially his deputy, Raincloud, but Darkstar refused to go back on his word. Each Clan set new border marks the following day, and SkyClan had to watch their rivals feast on prey that had once been theirs.

Seasons passed, and Twolegs began building new nests on SkyClan's borders. As their territory shrank on one side, their leader, Cloudstar, looked at the hunting grounds that had once belonged to them, and knew that those grounds would give his

Clan a chance of survival if Twolegs stole any more of their land. He launched an invasion with his warriors and tried to take back the territory by force. But ThunderClan was expecting this and fought back, hard, and with the strength of full-fed warriors.

Two Clans licked their wounds and told stories to their kits, stories that could not have been more different, on each side of the border. . . .

❁

The Victorious Clan

"Clanmates, we won!"

Redstar crossed the clearing in two bounds and leaped onto the Highrock. He gazed down at his Clan circling beneath him, purring and yowling with delight. The scratch on his muzzle, the ache in his hind leg where a SkyClan warrior had crushed it, the patch of fur missing from his flank: None of that mattered now. Victory was better than any herbs at making pain disappear.

Kestrelwing, the ThunderClan medicine cat, stood on tiptoe at the mouth of his den and called, "Any cats with injuries, come see me!"

A few warriors shuffled toward him, but most stayed, sharing their stories with the queens and elders who hadn't taken part in the battle. One gray tabby was dragged to the ground by a tumble of squeaking kits, who succeeded in flooring him when several SkyClan warriors dropping from trees had failed.

"Tell us about the battle!" the biggest kit begged.

"Were the SkyClan cats superbig and scary?" squealed another.

Nettleclaw shook his head. "No, but they were hungry, and that makes any enemy more dangerous."

"Not too dangerous for us!" chirped the first kit. "I bet you showed them who's the best around here!"

Nettleclaw let out a snort of amusement. "I guess we did, little one," he purred.

Redstar jumped down from Highrock, planning to see Kestrelwing once the first rush for treatment was over. His deputy, Seedpelt, padded up to him.

"Welcome back," she meowed, her eyes shining. "All was quiet while you were out."

Redstar nodded. "I thought it would be. SkyClan could barely muster enough warriors to take us on. They wouldn't have had any to spare to attack the camp. Thanks for staying behind, though. I know you would have liked to have been there."

"My turn will come," Seedpelt murmured. "Until then, I am honored to protect the Clan while you are not here."

A long-legged ginger cat passed them on his way to the fresh-kill pile. He flicked Redstar's shoulder with his tail as he drew level. "Well fought, old friend," he purred.

Redstar dipped his head. "Thank you, Amberclaw. You weren't too shabby yourself. Nice move with the sand-colored she-cat, I thought."

Redstar's brother paused. "Yes, she wasn't expecting me to dodge quite so quickly when she hopped out of that tree, was she? She didn't seem too happy about getting up afterward."

"Stupid furballs," Seedpelt snorted. "I don't know why they insist on flinging themselves out of trees all the time. Don't they realize we can see them up there, heaving about like great lumps of fluff?"

"Excuse me, Redstar, but are you going to stand there bleeding or would you like some cobweb on that wound?"

Kestrelwing was hovering at Redstar's shoulder with a pawful of white stuff. He patted it fussily against the leader's muzzle, making him sneeze.

"Enough!" Redstar ordered, shaking sticky strands out of his eyes. "See to the others first."

Kestrelwing pattered away, muttering, "Oh, yes, because Clan leaders have blood to spare, don't they?"

Gradually, the clearing quieted. The sky above the trees faded to pink, then gray, but the cats showed no inclination of going to bed. Warriors sat in groups, discussing the battle, reviewing what they had done well and moves that needed practice. Redstar joined them, praising and consoling, pointing out that whatever had happened, ThunderClan had won, and nothing else mattered. Kestrelwing met him as he was heading for his den.

"Have you seen the sky?" the medicine cat prompted. His eyes were shadowed with tiredness from treating all the injured warriors, but there was a gleam in them that spoke of more than a single victory.

Redstar looked up. The night sky was almost impossible to see behind the swath of sparkling stars. Silverpelt glowed brighter than a full moon, and the wind was full of the whispers of his ancestors, calling his name.

"StarClan approves, doesn't it?" he whispered to Kestrelwing.

The gray cat nodded. "You won this battle with the blessing of our ancestors," he agreed. "You are a hero in the stars already."

Redstar felt a warm glow of pride—and relief, too. "Then this means that the territory we fought over today belongs to ThunderClan by right. Darkstar's word stands, now and forever. It will never be given up!"

The Defeated Clan

C lanmates, we lost."

Cloudstar padded into the center of the camp, his head hanging with more than weariness. Every scrape on his pelt burned like fire, and his paws were numb from leaping onto the hard, dusty ground. "I'm so sorry," he murmured.

Birdflight trotted up to him, her swollen belly rolling with each stride, her amber eyes dark with concern. "You . . . you *lost?* But you said we had to win this battle!"

"Yes, we had to, but we didn't!" Cloudstar snarled. Then he took a step back. "I'm sorry. You're right; we should have won. We need that piece of territory to feed us."

His deputy, Buzzardtail, limped past, his tail dragging in the dirt. "Go straight to Fawnstep," Cloudstar ordered.

All around the clearing, queens and elders huddled around the returning warriors. They spoke so quietly, Cloudstar could hear a thrush warbling somewhere in the territory. *Brave, foolish bird*, he thought. *If you stay here, you'll be prey tomorrow.* There were so few birds left, he wondered if he should send a warrior now to catch it. But every cat fit enough to hunt had fought in the battle, and all had come back with injuries, from ripped ears to a broken leg, in Mousefang's case. That fox-hearted ThunderClan cat had jumped out of the way just as she dropped from the branch above him—StarClan knew how he'd heard her above the noise of the battle.

Maybe StarClan *did* know. But they weren't telling him. Cloudstar wondered if his warrior ancestors had even been watching today. It certainly hadn't felt as if they were on his side.

Birdflight nudged him gently. "You need to get that cut on your flank seen to," she prompted.

"Not yet," Cloudstar replied. "I must speak to the Clan first, tell them that we're not giving up after one defeat."

He clawed his way up to the branch in the gnarled thorn tree where he addressed his Clanmates. The branch seemed higher than usual, and his hind leg exploded with pain when he tried to push himself up. Once, he could stare into the trees from here and only guess where his territory ended. Now the half-built Twoleg nests loomed beyond the thin screen of branches, red and hard and threatening. They had swallowed up almost half of SkyClan's territory already. When would they stop?

A cough below him brought his attention back to his Clanmates, who had gathered under the tree. The cats who had fought alongside him wore empty, defeated expressions; the only

signs of hope were in the eyes of the cats who had stayed behind, the queens and the elders. Cloudstar hadn't left a single warrior to defend the camp, praying that ThunderClan had no interest in launching a separate attack. His hunch had paid off; he told himself that the losses could have been worse.

"Cats of SkyClan!" He made himself stand straight and tall on his branch, and tried to sound like a leader whose courage hadn't wavered with this defeat. "The reason we lost today is that ThunderClan fought harder and better. They wanted victory more than we did."

There were a few looks of surprise from his exhausted warriors, but others nodded and twitched their tails, as if they were feeling guilty for letting their Clanmates down. Something stabbed deep inside Cloudstar's heart—he knew his warriors had given everything they could, but they were outnumbered, hungry, and exhausted from too many fruitless hunting patrols. Yet he had to appeal to their sense of loyalty and honor to keep them fighting for their Clanmates.

"I don't blame any of you. All I ask is that you look at what you did today, and see if you could have done any more. If the answer is yes, then there will be other battles, other chances to prove what it means to be a SkyClan warrior."

Already the cats below him were lifting their heads, summoning up the remnants of their battered pride and thinking ahead to future wars.

Cloudstar finished: "SkyClan will take back what is rightfully ours. We will seize that territory from those ThunderClan thieves!"

A few reedy cheers rose from the listening cats. Cloudstar let out a sigh of relief. He had not lost his warriors' faith. Sometimes it felt as if that were all that was left of his leadership. He lowered himself carefully down the trunk and limped to Fawnstep's den.

He needed cobwebs, marigold, comfrey to ease his bruises—but not poppy seed. He would not take the coward's escape into sleep tonight. Instead, he would lie awake and figure out a better way to attack ThunderClan, a different strategy that would give his warriors the advantage from the beginning.

"Cloudstar! Cloudstar, wake up!"

A wet muzzle was thrust into Cloudstar's ear. Grunting, he swatted it aside and sat up. Through the branches of his den, he could see the sky turning milky with dawn, but it was dark enough that the stars still glittered overhead. *Are you still watching, StarClan? Any words of wisdom now?*

"Cloudstar, I have to talk to you!"

A blast of hot, herb-scented breath revealed that the intruder in Cloudstar's den was Fawnstep, the medicine cat.

"What is it?" Cloudstar growled. "Is Birdflight having her kits?" He jumped up, suddenly wide-awake. "Is she all right? Do you need me to fetch herbs?"

"Sit down," hissed Fawnstep. "Or you'll wake every cat in the Clan. Birdflight is fine. Her kits will be here in the next quarter moon, but not tonight. She's sleeping peacefully in the nursery."

She shuffled farther into the den and sat down. Her pale brown fur was just visible against the leaves, and her eyes gleamed when she turned her head toward him.

"I've had a dream," she began. Her voice was higher-pitched than usual, and Cloudstar recognized another scent beneath the herb-dust clinging to her pelt: fear.

"I'm sure StarClan was showing me the future. Not far off— Birdflight was there with your kits, and they were still very small."

"But strong?" Cloudstar interrupted. "There's nothing wrong with them, is there?"

Fawnstep shook her head. "No, your kits looked . . . healthy."

Cloudstar didn't like the way she had paused, but he let her go on.

The medicine cat took a deep breath. "SkyClan was leaving the forest. I . . . I think we were at a Gathering. The other Clans were there. They were watching us go."

"What? That's absurd!" Cloudstar lashed his tail. "This is our territory!"

Fawnstep gazed at him, and Cloudstar winced at the sorrow in her eyes. "You don't understand," she meowed gently. "There was no territory left. Not for us. The Twolegs had taken it all, and we had nowhere else to go."

A crack opened in Cloudstar's heart, and for a moment he couldn't breathe. He didn't feel surprise, just sadness, and shame that he couldn't have saved his Clan. Was this how his leadership would end? With SkyClan destroyed, hounded out of the forest like a mangy fox?

Fawnstep rested her tail on his shoulder. "I'm so sorry, Cloudstar. You should not have lost that battle. It is a defeat that we cannot survive."

CONCLUSION:
ONESTAR'S FAREWELL

✤

hello, kittypets? Ah, there you are. I wondered where you'd gone. Did you get lost in these bushes? The island's bigger than it looks from the shore, isn't it? Follow me back to the clearing. We're leaving now. We'll take you as far as our border; then you must go home. You can find your way on your own, can't you? Good.

Did you learn everything you wanted to know about battles? I've heard some stories tonight that were new to me, I must say. What was Cedarheart talking about? There are rumors that he knows more about the history of the Clans than any other cat, but he's never shared anything with me.

Battle is not always the answer, but it is part of our heritage, the legacy passed to us by our warrior ancestors, as well as the path to our future. Some questions can only lead to conflict; all challenges deserve a brave, carefully planned response. As long as we fight with honor, courage, and respect for our enemies, the legacy of battle deserves to survive. We will continue to pass on our skills to the new apprentices, then watch as they train the next generation. Heroes will be celebrated, the losing side condemned to dust in our memories. This is what it means to be a warrior: to be proud of our legacy, of the battles that we have fought and that our ancestors fought on our behalf.

For as long as the fire burns in our blood, warrior Clans will fight.

Turn the page to play . . .

Visit www.warriorcats.com
*to download game rules, character sheets,
a practice mission, and more!*

Written by Stan! • Art by James L. Barry

THE DELUGE

Whatever the previous adventure you played, consider that three moons have passed since then. Determine what age that makes all of the cat characters (including one belonging to the person who will take the first turn as Narrator) and use the information found in the "Improving Your Cat" section of Chapter Four in the game rules to make the necessary improvements.

Unless you are the first person who will act as Narrator in this adventure, you should stop reading here. The information beginning in the next paragraph is for the Narrator only.

The Adventure Begins

Hello, Narrator! It's time to begin playing "The Deluge." Make sure all the players have their character sheets, the correct number of chips, a piece of paper, and a pencil. Remember that the point of the game is to have fun, so don't be afraid to go slow, keep the players involved, and refer to the rules if you aren't sure exactly what should happen next.

When you're ready, begin with **1** below.

1. Gray Skies, Wet Fur

Special Note: Some of the action in "The Deluge" depends on what Clans the players' cats belong to. The text below assumes they are from different Clans and that they need a special reason to be hunting together. If, however, they are all from the same Clan, some of the details in this scene will be unnecessary. Improvise where needed to make the description suit the situation.

Read Aloud: "Rain. In times of drought it seemed like there could be no such thing as too much rain. But it's been nearly a moon since any cat has seen more than a fleeting glimpse of the sky or the stars, and it's been raining practically nonstop for days."

Narrator Tips: This adventure takes place some time either before or after the drought the Clans experience in *Omen of the Stars #1: The Fourth Apprentice*. It doesn't affect the story either way, but you may want to decide when exactly these events occur, just so your players have a better idea how they fit in with the main Warriors storyline.

Explain to the players that the rain has made things uncomfortable for all the Clans. It's forced prey to stay in their dens, nests, and burrows as much as possible, which in turn is making it difficult for the Clans to find sufficient fresh-kill. Things are so bad, in fact, that StarClan has sent dreams to several cats telling them that it is important to send some warriors deeper into the forest to hunt. (If any of the players' cats have the Interpret Dreams Knack, they may be among those to whom StarClan has spoken.) The players' cats are those who have been selected for this assignment. If the players' cats are from different Clans, you can tell them that StarClan has talked about the need for all four Clans to work together in order to make it through this deluge.

Allow the players' cats to ask questions about and prepare themselves for the trip. There really aren't any particular details that you need to give them (though you can improvise any that you like). The whole goal is for them to spend a day or two hunting farther up on the hill in the deep woods and to bring the fresh-kill back for all the Clans to share. The cats may want to take some traveling herbs before they go, and as long as it seems reasonable, let them.

Nothing of significance happens during the first day's travel up the hill, but you can improvise some details if you like. Be sure to emphasize the rain, which varies in intensity from drizzle to downpour but never stops completely. Also note that the cats do not see or scent any prey along their journey.

The next day, the rain is as light as it's been in a long time—a fine mist even lighter than a sprinkle—but it's still there. There are also two sets of fresh tracks in the mud, each moving in a different direction.

To find out more, the cats can attempt See Checks, but not Smell Checks (the rain still makes it too difficult to get details that way), to get more information about the tracks. Knacks like Animal Lore and Track can be used to augment these Checks.

Any cat whose Check totals 5 or higher recognizes one of the sets of tracks as definitely having been made by a rabbit and thinks the other is probably a rabbit, too, only bigger. With a total of 8 or higher, the cat recognizes the second set is not made by a rabbit but still isn't certain what animal made it. With a total of 10 or higher, the cat knows that the second set of tracks was made by a fox.

What Happens Next: Since the cats are on a hunting mission, they need to follow one of the sets of tracks. If they don't care which set they follow, or if none of them got a 5 or higher on their Skill Checks, you should decide which tracks they will follow.

If the cats follow the rabbit tracks, continue with **5**.

If the cats follow the fox tracks, continue with **14**.

2. A Slippery Adversary

Read Aloud: "Hot on the trail, you burst through a dense thicket of brush and . . . find yourself back at the very spot from which you started. Somewhere along the line you must have made a wrong turn."

Narrator Tips: The cats are right back where they began with nothing more to show for their efforts than an increased appreciation for how clever their target is. They only have a few choices at this point.

The most obvious choice is to get back on the trail and continue trying to track down the creature that made these tracks (which they may or may not realize is a fox). If they do this, the process is very similar to the one they just finished (in scene **14**), except that the knowledge they've gained gives them an edge. This time, they only need a Check total of 7 or higher for success, and they only need four successful Checks to correctly follow the trail. However, as before, if they get three failures first, they followed the wrong trail.

Alternatively, if they haven't yet followed the other set of tracks (the ones that obviously were made by rabbits), they might decide to let the mystery go in favor of hunting for fresh-kill—the reason they're on this mission in the first place. This course of action is also possible following a second failure in tracking the fox, but only if they haven't exhausted their rabbit-hunting possibilities (as described in scene **8**).

It they've already done their hunting, though, they may instead decide that getting their catch back to the Clans is more important than solving this mystery. They will still be able to report that there is a strange creature roaming not far from the Clan territories (which is certain to make the Clan leaders a little nervous).

What Happens Next: If the cats succeeded in following the trail, continue with **9**.

If the cats decide to take the rabbits they've already caught and head home, this is the end of the chapter. Pass the adventure to the next Narrator and tell him or her to continue with **12**.

If the cats decide to investigate the rabbit tracks, continue with **5**.

If the cats failed for a second time to follow the trail and cannot do any more hunting, tell the players that their cats have lost the scent and cannot find it again—the only option is for them to head home. This is the end of the chapter. Pass the adventure to the next Narrator and tell him or her to continue with **12** and to note that the cats failed twice at this task.

3. Looking for Advice

Read Aloud: "It's easy to skirt the edge of ShadowClan territory—the borders are marked quite clearly. All Clans are protective of their territory, but ShadowClan often seems to be the most firm in that protection. Hopefully one of the other Clan leaders will know how best to deal with this situation."

Narrator Tips: Help guide the players' cats to talk about the situation. With the danger so imminent, is it really right to walk away from ShadowClan, even if it is to seek advice? Should the group risk the anger of ShadowClan and bring them the message directly? It's a difficult question, one with no absolute right answer. But the discussion can be interesting in itself.

After the players have had a chance to talk about the issue, have all the cats make Listen Checks. Anyone whose total is 7 or higher hears a deep, wet "schloomph" sound in the distance. Clearly at least one of the ponds has collapsed. There may be a flash flood headed down the hill right now!

What Happens Next: The group has a difficult decision to make. Will they go into ShadowClan territory to help save them from the flash flood or will they continue on their original course?

If the group decides to stay on their original course, continue with **20**.

If the group decides to cross the border into ShadowClan territory to try to help, continue with **11**.

4. Carried Away

Read Aloud: "You're tumbling head over tail and rolling downhill in a slosh of water and mud."

Narrator Tips: One or more of the cats has been caught in the collapse of the pond and the resulting flash flood. Any cats in this predicament immediately take damage that causes them to lose 3 chips. Then they must make a Swim Check to get their heads above the water. If this Check has a total of 7 or higher they succeed, otherwise they lose an additional 2 chips.

Being caught in the flashflood uses a system of rounds just like fighting does (see Chapter Five of the game rules for details). In order to escape the flash flood, a cat needs to be pulled to safety by someone who is not currently in the water. To do that, a cat that is safely on land must make a Swat Check with a total of 5 or higher. Each cat on dry land can only attempt to pull one cat from the water each round. At the end of the first round, the cats who are still in the water must make another Swim Check, as described above; then a new round begins.

This continues for three rounds or until either all of the cats are rescued from the flash flood or knocked out from their ordeal.

What Happens Next: If all the cats were rescued from the flash flood, continue with **13**.

If any of the cats were knocked out by their ordeal, continue with **7**.

5. Rabbit Ears

Read Aloud: "The rabbit's tracks are not difficult to follow. Hopping through the mud leaves deep imprints. After scampering under some bushes and over a log, the tracks lead you to a small meadow where you don't just see one rabbit—you see several of them!"

Narrator Tips: The cats have followed their prey to an area where all the local rabbits feed. Many of the rabbits haven't had a decent meal in days because of the rains, so quite a few are here now, chewing contentedly on grass. There are enough rabbits that each cat can try to catch one on his or her own. The problem is, the ground is still soft and muddy.

Tell the players that the slippery conditions will make it more difficult than usual to sneak up on and catch their prey (don't tell them the details described below; they only need to know that it will be more difficult in general). Tell them also that it will be easier for them to catch prey in these poor conditions if they hunt in pairs.

Hunting is described in Chapter Five of the game rules, and those basic rules will apply to this scene. However, because of the soggy state of the ground, things will be a little different.

Because all the cats are hunting in the same area, you should have them all hunt at the same time. If one cat attacks a rabbit, all the other rabbits in the area will flee. So you should first have all of the cats make their Sneak Checks, and then have them all make Pounce Checks at the same time.

Cats who are hunting alone must make a Sneak Check with a total of 10 or higher in order to succeed at stalking their prey. Cats who are working in pairs should each make a separate Sneak Check, then add their totals together. If their combined total is 14 or higher, they succeed as a team. For every cat or pair of cats that fails their Sneak Check, they were not sneaky enough to trick the rabbits and you'll have to increase the difficulty of the Pounce Checks below by +2. So if one cat or team failed, the difficulty for all the cats is increased by +2; if two failed, the increase is +4; and so on.

When all the cats have finished making their Sneak Checks, it is time for them to try to nab their intended prey. Have all the cats make Pounce Checks. The difficulty of this Check is based on the rabbits' Jump scores. All of the rabbits have a Jump score of 9, but this may be increased if any of the cats fail to be sneaky enough. Cats who are hunting alone have only one chance to catch their rabbit—if they miss, it gets away. Cats that are hunting in pairs may each make a Pounce attempt, so even if one is unlucky, the other may still succeed.

If the cats have successfully caught rabbits, they must Bite in order to finish them. The Bite Check is made against the rabbit's strength of 3. Multiple cats can bite a single rabbit, so even if a cat failed to catch one of her own, she can still help to bring down another one. If a rabbit takes 4 chips worth of damage, it is killed.

Any rabbit that is still alive after all the cats have made their attacks will try to escape. The cat (or cats) holding it must make Wrestling Checks to keep their grip and can perform another round of Bite attacks. If the Wrestling Check is 5 or higher, the cats are successful. If not, the rabbit escapes and dashes into a nearby burrow before the cats can pounce again.

What Happens Next: If at least one rabbit was caught, continue with **10.**

If all of the rabbits got away, continue with **8.**

6. Talking to the Shadows

Read Aloud: "Ratscar looks at you suspiciously. 'What have you got to say that's so important?'"

Narrator Tips: Remember that any of the players' cats that belong to ShadowClan get bonuses to some of their Checks (as described in scene **17**). Under normal circumstances, that would mean that the ShadowClan patrol cats would automatically believe what the players' cats said—members of the same Clan trust one another. But the presence of cats from other Clans puts the members of the patrol in a very aggressive frame of mind. The fact that a member of ShadowClan is standing with these other cats instead of his or her Clanmates has clouded the patrolling cats' judgment and they must be convinced to listen to reason.

Let the players' cats lead the conversation, giving them sufficient time to explain themselves. The cats of ShadowClan may be suspicious, but clearly something important must be happening if this group so brazenly crossed their border without a full war party.

The scene will center around you improvising Ratscar's and the other ShadowClan cats' reactions and responses to what the players' cats say. It may also involve the players' cats making Spirit or Intelligence Checks (aided by Orate or Clan Lore) to try to find the right words to make their opponents understand the importance and danger of this moment. Such Checks are opposed by the ShadowClan cats' Spirit scores (and you can spend their Ability chips in the process if they are feeling particularly stubborn).

If the players' cats do well, it will make the ShadowClan cats more likely to trust them. If they do poorly, or purposely antagonize the patrol, the ShadowClan cats may decide that fighting is the better option.

After the conversation has gone on a little while, have all the cats (including the ShadowClan patrol) make Listen Checks. Any cat whose total is 7 or higher hears the deep, wet "schloomph" sound of the pools above collapsing. Any player's cat that hears this knows there is now a flash flood coming down the hill somewhere near here.

What Happens Next: If there is a breakdown of communications and the two sides are ready to begin fighting, continue with **18**.

If everyone failed the Listen Check, this is the end of the chapter. Hand the adventure to the next Narrator and tell him or her to continue with **15**.

If the cats know that the flash flood is coming, they can only brace themselves and continue to try to warn other members of ShadowClan of the impending danger. This is the end of the chapter. Hand the adventure to the next Narrator and tell him or her to continue with **11**.

7. Calamity!

Special Note: There is no Read Aloud text for this scene. It is a catchall scene for you to use if the cats' adventure comes to an unhappy and untimely conclusion. Use the information below to improvise suitable details.

Narrator Tips: Something the cats did has caused the adventure to come to an unhappy end. This may have been the result of poor planning or just bad luck. This scene is about providing a sense of completion (if not success) to the story. Below are notes to help you improvise scenes based on the most likely reasons for the cats ending up here.

Fighting the Fox: If the cats fought the fox and one or more cats were knocked out, the adventure has to conclude. Helping their fallen friend takes so much time that the group misses the opportunity to take part in the other chapters of this story. By the time the players' cats are able to get back down the hill, they find that a flash flood has swept through ShadowClan territory, injuring many cats and even killing a few. No blame is laid on the group—after all, the flood was not their fault—but let the players know that their cats have a nagging suspicion that they could have helped in some way. Perhaps next time, they will be more careful when going into battle.

Caught in a Flash Flood: The players' cats may end up here because one or more of them was knocked out by a flash flood. The first flash flood occurs during their hunting trip, and the results are similar to those described above—taking care of the fallen cat keeps the group out of the rest of the adventure. The other possibility is that the cats were caught in the climactic flash flood, in which case they've seen the adventure to its conclusion, but the injuries have kept the adventure from being counted as a success.

Fighting with ShadowClan: If two or more of the cats are knocked out in the fight with the ShadowClan warriors, the group is unable to help save any other cats from the flash flood. The flood is still not their fault, but they know that if they'd been able to get past the warriors' resistance, they could have prevented some of the injuries and death—perhaps all of it.

What Happens Next: Although they tried hard, the cats do *not* get any Experience rewards for this adventure. The group *can*, however, play the adventure again, hopefully changing some of their tactics so that they get a better result next time.

8. Empty Bellies

Read Aloud: "Blame it on the mud and muck. Blame it on the growling of your empty stomach. Blame it on bad luck. But whatever you blame it on, the rabbits got away. And, to make matters worse, it's started raining again."

Narrator Tips: The cats have failed to capture any rabbits, which means that they are completely failing in their mission. Although they are undoubtedly aware of it, remind the players that StarClan sent them on this mission specifically to get fresh-kill. Certainly, they will want another chance to hunt.

After failing once, the cats may wait along the meadow's edge until the rabbits return. There will be fewer of them (only half as many as there are players in the game), so the cats will have to team up. That's a good thing, though, because these rabbits will be even more difficult to catch than the first bunch. If this is the second time the cats have failed to capture any rabbits, then they are through hunting. The rabbits will not return for the rest of the day.

Alternatively, the cats may want to go investigate the other set of tracks they saw when they awoke this morning. Even though those tracks aren't rabbit tracks, maybe they'll lead to something interesting.

Finally, the cats may decide to give up. If this is the case, remind them that it will be an embarrassment to go back to their Clanmates without any fresh-kill. But if they're firm in their desire to give up, don't try to force them into a different course of action.

What Happens Next: If the cats get another chance to hunt, continue with **5**, but make all of the target numbers 2 points higher because the rabbits know there are cats around.

If the cats decide to go investigate the other set of tracks, continue with **14**.

If the cats decide to give up and go back down the hill to report their failure, this is the end of the chapter. Pass the adventure to the next Narrator and tell him or her to continue with **12**.

9. Fox Found

Read Aloud: "Hot on the trail, you burst through a final dense thicket of brush and find yourself face-to-face with a proud, russet-furred fox."

Narrator Tips: In point of fact, this is not a fox—it's a vixen (a female fox). As the Narrator you should know her background and motivation. This vixen has recently had a litter of pups and is out hunting so she can feed them. She saw the cats and laid this trail on purpose to lead them away from her den. Her main motivation is to either scare the cats away or to make them think her den is somewhere near here. Once one of those things is accomplished, she will sneak back to her pups to keep them warm and safe.

Of course, the cats do not have any way of knowing that. Here is what they can see and learn.

Rather than running any farther, the fox stands her ground and bares her teeth in a snarl. She seems to be daring the cats to come closer. If the players ask, their cats can learn some information by making the Skill Checks (all of which require a total of 7 or higher to succeed). An Animal Lore Check can tell them that this type of posturing is unusual for a fox—but no one really understands the behavior of foxes, so it's difficult to draw conclusions. A Smell Check can tell them that this is a female fox (a vixen) and that her fur carries the scent of at least three other foxes, though none of those foxes are in the area. A Ponder Check will tell them that although she has struck an aggressive stance, she doesn't seem ready to fight to the death—it may be possible to chase her away.

If the cats want to scare the vixen away by Hissing and Arching at her, have them make the appropriate Skill Checks. (Each cat may only perform one Check.) Add the results to get a group total. If this group total is 25 or higher, the vixen hisses back but then sprints into the woods. The cats can try to follow, but it soon becomes clear that she is running away from Clan territory as fast as she can and that it would likely take the cats hours to catch up with her.

If the group total is 23 or less, the cats have two choices—attack the vixen and hope to drive her off, or simply walk away and leave her alone.

If they decide to attack, their fighting will follow the standard rules (see Chapter Five of the game rules). The vixen has Ability scores of Strength 7, Intelligence 9, Spirit 11. Her Skills are Bite +4, Jump +4, Sneak +6. And she has the following Knacks: Alertness, Hide, and Dodge. She has the Ability chips and can spend them during battle just the way the players' cats can. You may want to write down the vixen's game stats on a piece of paper for easy reference during the fight.

The vixen will fight until she has taken 7 chips worth of damage. At that point she will run away as described above. It is possible, though not likely, that she will hurt the cats so badly that they must run away. If this happens, the vixen will let out one final hiss and then stalk proudly into the woods (and then, once she is out of sight of the cats, she will quickly dash off to the safety of her den).

When the encounter with the vixen is over, the cats have a few choices. They can go back and hunt for rabbits (unless that action is no longer an option for them, as described in scene **8**) or they can take what fresh-kill they've gathered and head for home.

What Happens Next: If one or more of the cats was knocked out in the fight with the vixen, continue with **7**.

If the cats decide to go hunting for rabbits, continue with **5**.

If the cats decide to head back down the hill toward home, this is the end of the chapter. Pass the adventure to the next Narrator and tell him or her to continue with **12**.

10. Fresh-kill!

Read Aloud: "You're a Clan cat, and that means that even though the hunt is successful, you can't eat until you've brought back food for the Clan. Still, the taste of the rabbit is sweet on your tongue and you know that, plump as it is, several cats will share this meal."

Narrator Tips: The cats have succeeded in getting some fresh-kill, so they have been at least partially successful in their mission. On the trip home, the most they will be able to carry is one rabbit each. Until they have that many rabbits, this is not a completely successful hunt and they cannot eat anything (you may want to remind them that they are feeling hungry). The question is: What do they want to do next?

The cats may want to hunt again, to get more food for the Clans—plus a little extra for themselves. On the other hand, they may want to take what they've got back to the Clan camps quickly. There's also a chance that, the hunt having been successful, they'll want to investigate the other set of tracks they saw when they woke up this morning.

Your job is simply to make sure that the players are aware of those choices. Whatever choice they make is up to them.

What Happens Next: If the players decide they want to hunt some more, they only have to wait a short while and rabbits will return to this meadow. Let them stalk and hunt again using the details in **5**.

If the players decide to investigate the other set of tracks, continue with **14**.

If the group decides to take the fresh-kill they have back down the hill to the Clans, this is the end of the chapter. Pass the adventure to the next Narrator and tell him or her to continue with **12**.

11. Here It Comes Again

Read Aloud: "A great, rushing wall of water tumbles down the hill at breakneck speed. It looks like a river that suddenly decided that this was a better course than the one it previously followed. You're not in its path, but farther down the hill you can see some cats who are."

Narrator Tips: If any of the players' cats belong to ShadowClan, they immediately recognize that the flash flood is headed very near their Clan's camp. Most of the queens, kits, and elders will be in that area and therefore in danger. If none of the players' cats come from ShadowClan, Ratscar will volunteer this information.

The flash flood narrowly misses the ShadowClan camp itself, but you can hear the yowls of cats that were caught in the waters and are being rushed off toward the Lake. All the warriors in the area rush off to help, so no one stands in the way of the players' cats. They can come in and help with the rescue efforts if they like. Alternatively, they can decide that the cats of ShadowClan deserve what they're getting for being so suspicious of cats who came here only to help.

What Happens Next: If the group decides to help the members of ShadowClan who are caught in the flash flood, continue with **16**.

If the group thinks that ShadowClan is just getting what it deserves, and walks away to leave them to their fate, continue with **20**.

12. An Unexpected Pond

Read Aloud: "As you make your way down the hill, you notice that the rain has finally stopped. This will make the trip home much more pleasant, and you think about that as you stop to get a drink from a small pond. Then you suddenly realize that this pond was not here during your trip up the hill yesterday."

Special Note: If the cats failed to catch any rabbits on this hunting mission, their hunger and sense of failure make this scene more difficult. Add +2 to all the target numbers in this scene. Additionally, if the cats tried to follow the fox's trail but failed twice, their sense of disappointment also increases the difficulty—add +1 to the target numbers. These conditions can be added together, so if they neither got any rabbits nor followed the fox, the target numbers in this scene all should be increased by a total of +3.

Narrator Tips: To figure out where this pond came from, one of the cats needs to make a Ponder Check with a total of 5 or higher. Getting that total lets the cat know that the pond is the result of the incredible amount of water from the recent rains. This is normally a small ravine, but it's filled with runoff water.

If the Ponder Check had a total of 7 or higher, the cat also realizes that this is a dangerous place. Because the ground is so muddy and the gathering water is so heavy, it's unlikely the ravine can withstand the pressure—the muddy sides are likely to collapse and send the water spilling down the hill.

If the Ponder Check had a total of 9 or higher, the cat realizes that this catastrophe is going to happen very soon.

Allow the cats a few moments to think about what they've realized, and to step away from the water's edge if they want to.

Just a few moments later there is a loud, wet "schloomph" sound and any cats that are still drinking from or standing next to the pond must make a Jump Check as the downhill side of the ravine collapses in a mudslide and the entire contents of the pond spill out at once.

What Happens Next: If any of the affected cats have a Jump Check total of 10 or lower, continue with **4**.

If all of the affected cats have a Jump Check total of 11 or higher (or none of them were standing close enough to be affected), continue with **13**.

13. Impending Doom

Read Aloud: "Where just a few minutes ago there was a pond, now there is nothing but a swath of mud and slime that trails straight down the hill for as far as you can see."

Narrator Tips: Use the first part of this scene to make sure the cats understand how much damage the flash flood just did. The solid wall of water suddenly rushing down the hillside knocked down some saplings, whisked away loose branches and small rocks, and even pried a few large rocks loose from the ground, sending everything tumbling toward the bottom of the hill.

Have each of the cats make a Ponder Check—let them know that the Clan Lore Knack can be helpful in this activity, if they want to use it. Those who get a result of 8 or better are relieved to know for certain that directly below them on the hill is an area that is outside of the Clan territories. They can continue their trip home.

A while later, though, the cats come across another pond like the one they just saw. But not just one—they see a close grouping of three ponds in a row leading down the hill. The cats realize that when the walls of these ponds collapse, the devastation will be three times more powerful than what they just witnessed.

Have each of the cats make another Ponder Check—again, the Clan Lore Knack can be used. Any cat who belongs to ShadowClan gets a bonus of +4 to this Check. Those who get a total of 6 or lower believe that these ponds are also above a safe area that the cats don't frequent. Those who get a total of 9 or less know that this area is directly above ShadowClan territory, but believe it is away from the area where most of the cats live and hunt. Those who get a total of.10 or higher know that the area directly below these ponds is very close to the ShadowClan camp.

The question is: What will the group do with the knowledge they have gained? Normally, ShadowClan is fiercely protective of their land and entering it without invitation is dangerous. But the danger is real and could strike at any time. Perhaps one of the other Clan leaders will have a better idea of what to do. But taking the time to go ask is risky—the ponds could collapse at any moment.

What Happens Next: If the group decides to head into ShadowClan territory to warn them of the danger, continue with **17**.

If the group decides to continue back to one of the other Clan camps to talk to that Clan's leader, continue with **3**.

14. A Winding Trail

Read Aloud: "It's clear these aren't rabbit tracks—no rabbit was ever as clever or determined as the creature you're now following. The trail goes through bushes and over rocks; it speeds up, slows down, and doubles back across its own path repeatedly. Whoever made these tracks is a sly character indeed."

Narrator Tips: Whether or not the cats know these are fox tracks, they at least know that they're following a clever creature. Improvise a description for where the trail goes, and at several points have the players choose one of their cats to make a See or Smell Check to stay on the trail (the Track Knack can be used on these Checks). Do not let the same cat make all the Checks—this requires a team effort.

If a Check has a total of 8 or higher, it counts as a success, 7 or lower and it's a failure. If the group gets four successes before it gets three failures, it has succeeded in running down the creature. If the group gets three failures first, it has followed the wrong trail.

What Happens Next: If the cats succeeded in catching up with the creature, continue with **9**.

If the cats followed the wrong trail, continue with **2**.

15. Gone in a Flash

Read Aloud: "You hear another, louder sloshing sound and then notice a literal wall of water racing down the hill toward you."

Narrator Tips: If the group ends up in this scene it is because the players missed the warning signs that a flash flood is imminent. Getting out of the way at this point will be very difficult. Any cat who wants to try to avoid the water must make a Jump Check (using the Dodge Knack will be very helpful).

A Jump Check with a total of 12 or higher will allow a cat to get out of the way of the flash flood. Any lower and the cat is swept away by the water.

Cats caught in the flash flood immediately take damage that causes them to lose 4 chips. Then they must make a Swim Check to get their heads above the water. If this Check has a total of 7 or higher they succeed, otherwise they lose an additional 2 chips.

In order to escape the flash flood, a cat needs to be pulled to safety by someone who is not currently in the water (if all the cats failed, there is no one to save them so they will just be carried away by the flood). To do that, a cat must make a Swat Check with a total of 5 or higher. Each cat on dry land can only attempt to pull one cat from the water each round. (Being involved with the flash flood uses a system of rounds just like fighting does—see Chapter Five of the game rules for details.) At the end of the round, the cats who are still in the water automatically take 1 chip worth of damage, and then must make another Swim Check, as described above; then a new round begins.

This continues for five rounds or until either all of the players' cats are rescued from the flash flood or knocked out from their ordeal.

What Happens Next: If two or more of the players' cats were knocked out by the flash flood, continue with **7**.

If the five rounds of the flood pass and fewer than two of the cats have been knocked out, continue with **19**.

If all of the players' cats are rescued from the flash flood, continue with **16**.

16. To the Rescue

Read Aloud: "You've rarely seen such chaos—water rushing through the middle of a Clan territory, cats yowling for help as they try to keep their heads above water, everyone who's not in the water running around trying to save some cat who is. There's no sensible place to start, you just have to dig in and help any way you can."

Narrator Tips: Everywhere the players' cats look there are ShadowClan cats who need help. The flood will last for five rounds, using a system of rounds just like fighting does (see Chapter Five of the game rules for details). Rescuing a cat from the water simply requires a Swat Check, but the difficulty changes depending on what kind of cat you are attempting to rescue. Each round, have every player say whether his or her cat is going to try to rescue a kit, a warrior, or an elder.

Rescuing a warrior or an elder requires a Swat Check with a total of 5 or higher. Rescuing kits is more difficult because they are so small. To rescue a kit, a cat must have a Swat Check with a total of 7 or higher. In addition, if the Swat Check fails, the cat must immediately make a Focus Check to avoid losing his or her balance. If the Focus Check is 5 or lower, the cat falls into the water.

Whether or not the players' cats can be said to have been "successful" at helping ShadowClan depends on how many cats they rescued. For every warrior or elder the cats rescue, they get 1 point. For every kit they rescue, the cats get 2 points

What Happens Next: If any of the players' cats fall into the water, continue with **15**.

If the flooding ends and the players' cats have rescued fewer than 15 points worth of ShadowClan cats, continue with **20**.

If the flooding ends and the players' cats have rescued 15 or more points worth of ShadowClan cats, continue with **19**.

17. Border Patrol

Read Aloud: "At first it's difficult to tell that you're in ShadowClan territory. This high up the hill, it looks like any other stretch of woods and there are no scent marks to identify the place. But as you get lower, the trees begin to grow closer together, making it feel like dusk despite the fact that it's the middle of the day. And a scent becomes clear—a scent that says, 'This is ShadowClan territory! Go away!'"

Special Note: Although ShadowClan as a whole can sometimes be secretive and difficult to deal with, they are not by any means evil cats. In fact, the individual cats of ShadowClan are as varied as those of any Clan. It is entirely possible that some, or even all, of the players in your game have cats who are from ShadowClan. If so, these cats get a +4 bonus to any Intelligence, Spirit, Focus, Hiss, or Ponder Check made while interacting with other ShadowClan cats in this adventure.

Narrator Tips: As the cats get closer to the bottom of the hill and the Lake, they enter the most populated part of ShadowClan territory. It's always nerve-wracking going uninvited into another Clan's territory, and ShadowClan has a reputation for being especially protective of its borders.

The land itself seems well suited for ShadowClan. The trees grow close together, blocking out the sky and casting shadows everywhere. A cat who knew the territory well could be hiding nearby and a stranger would never even know it.

Do what you can to play up the mystery and danger of the scene, and then have a patrol of ShadowClan cats arrive, seeming one instant to be a part of the shadows and the next stepping out for all to see. There are a number of cats in the patrol equal to the number of players' cats (not counting the Narrator's cat). They are bold and aggressive and the largest of them, Ratscar, steps forward and challenges the players' cats. He demands to know what they are doing in ShadowClan territory and ordering them to leave immediately. The ShadowClan cats arch their backs and hiss, but do not actually attack. It is clear, though, that they are challenging the players' cats to make the first move.

What Happens Next: The next step is up to the players and how their cats choose to react.

If they want to talk to the ShadowClan cats to tell them about the danger, continue with **6**.

If they want to accept the ShadowClan cats' challenge and start fighting, continue with **18**.

18. Border Skirmish

Read Aloud: "'Now we see your treachery!' yells Ratscar. 'ShadowClan, attack!'"

Narrator Tips: This scene centers around a battle between the players' cats and the ShadowClan patrol (and uses the standard fighting rules as described in Chapter Five of the game rules). There is one member of the patrol for each of the players' cats (not counting the Narrator's). All of the ShadowClan cats have the same game statistics.

ShadowClan Patrol Cat: 20 moons old; Strength 6, Intelligence 3, Spirit 1; *Skills:* Arch +1, Jump +2, Sneak +2, Swat +2; *Knacks:* Belly Rake, Leap, Mighty Swat, Stalk, Track, Yowl.

You may want to write down the ShadowClan cats' game stats and track each of them separately on a piece of paper for easy reference during the fight.

After three rounds of fighting, have all the cats (including the ShadowClan patrol) make Listen Checks. Any cat whose total is 7 or higher hears the deep, wet "schloomph" sound of the pools above collapsing. Any player's cat who hears this knows there is a flash flood coming down the hill somewhere near here. The ShadowClan cats are a little worried by that strange sound but seem ready to go on fighting.

What Happens Next: If two or more of the players' cats were knocked out during the fight, continue with **7**.

If the cats decide to go on fighting, let them do so for one more round, then the chapter ends. Hand the adventure to the next Narrator and tell him or her to continue with **15**.

If the cats decide to stop fighting and try to warn other members of ShadowClan of the impending danger, this is the end of the chapter. Hand the adventure to the next Narrator and tell him or her to continue with **11**.

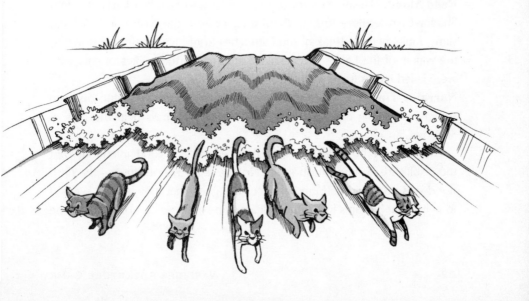

19. Here Comes the Sun

Read Aloud: "The next morning, representatives from all the Clans come into ShadowClan territory to help them recover from the flash flood. A long, slimy, foul-smelling streak of mud stretches from high on the hill down to the waters of the Lake, and there are branches and large rocks strewn all about. Only a few cats were hurt, though, and no one was killed, so it is not an exaggeration to say that a tragedy was averted—thanks in good part to your actions."

Narrator Tips: ShadowClan will not let the other Clans spend very much time here, not wanting them to learn too much about their territory. But it is important for them to prove that the flash flood has not weakened their Clan in any way—they are still as strong and capable of defending themselves as ever.

Blackstar, the ShadowClan leader, will give a brief statement of thanks to the players' cats, admitting that if not for their efforts the situation would have been much worse. The members of the other Clans might be more effusive with their praise.

What Happens Next: The players' cats should be proud of what they accomplished. But the nature of life as a warrior is that there is always another calamity waiting to happen. And, as good a job as the group did here, they should know that they'll have to do even better next time. Because it is a warrior's job to not just protect his or her Clan from one threat but from *all* of them!

20. Not Good Enough

Read Aloud: "The next morning, representatives of all the Clans come into ShadowClan territory to help them recover from the flash flood. A long, slimy, foul-smelling streak of mud stretches from high on the hill down to the waters of the Lake, and scattered around are the bodies of cats who were killed in this tragic event."

Narrator Tips: The players' cats have ended up in this scene because somewhere along the way they did not do enough to help the cats of ShadowClan.

It's entirely possible that they proceeded with good intentions, but the results are no less catastrophic. No one really blames them—the flash flood was not their fault, and chances are good that they at least wanted to help—but it seems likely that at least some of those hurt or killed by the waters could have been saved if the players' cats had been more deeply involved. If they were helping to rescue drowning cats, but didn't succeed in rescuing very many, some members of ShadowClan might think that the group wasn't trying hard enough.

On the other hand, it may be that the cats chose to ignore the problem because of some bias against ShadowClan. If this is the case, or if the players seem too unaffected by this tragedy, have a cat who they respect—perhaps their Clan leader—come over and talk to them about the events. Have that cat focus on the fact that part of the warrior code is to protect kits, no matter what Clan they belong to, and that can easily be imagined to mean any Clan cat who is helpless and in danger. The Clans may sometimes be at odds, but they must act together for the good of all if they are to survive the many dangers of the world.

What Happens Next: This is the end of the adventure, and it is not a good end. Although they tried hard, the cats do *not* get any Experience rewards for this adventure. The group *can*, however, play the adventure again, hopefully changing some of their tactics so that they get a better result next time.

AFTER THE ADVENTURE

After the last scene of the adventure has been played, the game itself is not necessarily over. There still are a few things you can do if the players want to keep at it.

Play It Again

Maybe you just want to try the whole thing a second time, starting back at the beginning or perhaps picking up somewhere in the middle where it feels like things went wrong. In either case, your cat would be right back where he or she was and have another chance to try to find a more favorable outcome.

One of the great things about storytelling games is that you can always tell the story again. And, since some of the group's actions can be strongly affected by how they did when they were hunting and tracking, they may want to go back and try putting more effort and emphasis in excelling during those scenes.

Plus, depending on how they handled the interaction with Ratscar and his ShadowClan patrol, they may want to see what happens if they try a different tactic. Playing again will let everyone see all the parts of the story and give other players the chance to try their hands at being the Narrator.

Experience

If the cats completed the adventure successfully, then they all get Experience rewards. It is important to note, though, that each cat can only get experience from this adventure *once*! If you play through and successfully finish the adventure several times, your cat only gains the rewards listed below after the *first* time he or she completes the adventure.

If you use different cats each time, though, each one can get the Experience rewards. The rule is *not* that a player can only get experience once, it's that a *cat* can.

Age: Although the action in this adventure clearly all happens over the course of a handful of days, the presumption is that this is the most interesting and exciting thing that happens to your cat during the whole of that moon. Increase your cat's age by 2 moons and make any appropriate improvements described in Chapter Four of the game rules.

Skill: On top of the improvements your cat gets from aging, he or she also can gain 1 level in one of the following Skills: Focus, Ponder, Swat, or Swim.

Knack: For having such close interactions with the members of ShadowClan and spending time in their territory, your cat also gains 1 level of the Clan Lore Knack.

More adventures can be found at the back of each novel in the Omen of the Stars series, and you can find extra information at the warriorcats. com website.

More adventures can be found at the back of each novel in the Omen of the Stars series, and you can find extra information at the warriorcats.com website.

Turn the page for a sneak peek at

SUPER EDITION

WARRIORS

SKYCLAN'S DESTINY

Many moons ago, five warrior Clans shared the forest in peace. But as Twolegs encroached on the cats' territories, the warriors of SkyClan were forced to abandon their home and try to forge a new life far away. Eventually, the Clan disbanded—forgotten by all until Firestar was sent on a quest to reunite its descendants and return SkyClan to its former glory.

Now, with Leafstar in place as leader, SkyClan is thriving. But threats continue to plague the Clan, and as dissent grows from within, Leafstar must face the one question she dreads: Is SkyClan meant to survive?

CHAPTER 1

❧

Floodwater thundered down the gorge, chasing a wall of uprooted trees
and bushes as if they were the slenderest twigs. Leafstar stood
at the entrance to her den and watched in horror as the current foamed and swirled among the rocks, mounting higher
and higher. Rain lashed the surface from bulging black clouds
overhead.

Water gurgled into Echosong's den; though the SkyClan
leader strained her eyes through the stormy darkness, she
couldn't see what had happened to the medicine cat. A cat's
shriek cut through the tumult of the water and Leafstar spotted the Clan's two elders struggling frantically as they were
swept out of their den. The two old cats flailed on the surface
for a heartbeat and then vanished.

Cherrytail and Patchfoot, heading down the trail with
fresh-kill in their jaws, halted in astonishment when they saw
the flood. They spun around and fled up the cliff, but the
water surged after them and carried them yowling along the
gorge. Leafstar lost sight of them as a huge tree, its roots high
in the air like claws, rolled between her and the drowning
warriors.

Great StarClan, help us! Leafstar prayed. *Save my Clan!*

Already the floodwater was lapping at the entrance to the nursery. A kit poked its nose out and vanished back inside with a frightened wail. Leafstar bunched her muscles, ready to leap across the rocks and help, but before she could move, a wave higher than the rest licked around her and caught her up, tossing her into the river alongside the splintered trees.

Leafstar fought and writhed against the smothering water, gasping for breath. She coughed as something brittle jabbed inside her open mouth. She opened her eyes and spat out a frond of dried bracken. Her nest was scattered around her den and there were deep claw marks in the floor where she had struggled with the invisible wave. Flicking off a shred of moss that was clinging to one ear, she sat up, panting.

Thank StarClan, it was only a dream!

The SkyClan leader stayed where she was until her heart-beat slowed and she had stopped trembling. The flood had been so real, washing away her Clanmates in front of her eyes. . . .

Sunlight was slanting through the entrance to her den; with a long sigh of relief, Leafstar tottered to her paws and padded onto the ledge outside. Down below, the river wound peacefully between the steep cliffs that enclosed the gorge. As sunhigh approached, light gleamed on the surface of the water and soaked into Leafstar's brown-and-cream fur; she relaxed her shoulders, enjoying the warmth and the sensation of the gentle breeze that ruffled her pelt.

"It was only a dream," she repeated to herself, pricking her ears at the twittering of birds in the trees at the top of the gorge. "Newleaf is here, and SkyClan has survived."

A warm glow of satisfaction flooded through her as she recalled that only a few short moons ago she had been nothing more than Leaf. She had been a loner, responsible for no cat but herself. Then Firestar had appeared: a leader of a Clan from a distant forest, with an amazing story of a lost Clan who had once lived here in the gorge. Firestar had gathered loners and kittypets to revive SkyClan; most astonishing of all, Leaf had been chosen to lead them.

"I'll never forget that night when the spirits of my ancestors gave me nine lives and made me Leafstar," she murmured. "My whole world changed. I wonder if you still think about us, Firestar," she added. "I hope you know that I've kept the promises I made to you and my Clanmates."

Shrill meows from below brought the she-cat back to the present. The Clan was beginning to gather beside the Rockpile, where the underground river flowed into the sunlight for the first time. Shrewtooth, Sparrowpelt, and Cherrytail were crouched down, eating, not far from the fresh-kill pile. Shrewtooth gulped his mouse down quickly, casting suspicious glances at the two younger warriors. Leafstar remembered how a border patrol had caught the black tom spying on the Clan two moons ago, terrified and half-starving. They had persuaded him to move into the warriors' den, but he was still finding it hard to fit into Clan life.

I'll have to do something to make him understand that he is among friends now, Leafstar decided. *He's more nervous than a cornered mouse.*

The two Clan elders, Lichenfur and Tangle, were sharing tongues on a flat rock warmed by the sun. They looked content; Tangle was a bad-tempered old rogue who stopped in the gorge now and again to eat before going back to his den in the forest, but he seemed to get on fine with Lichenfur, and Leafstar hoped she would convince him to stay permanently in the camp.

Lichenfur had lived alone in the woods farther up the gorge, aware of the new Clan but staying clear of them. She had almost died when she had been caught in a fox trap, until a patrol had found her and brought her back to camp for healing. After that she had been glad to give up the life of a loner. "She has wisdom to teach the Clan," Leafstar mewed softly from the ledge. "Every Clan needs its elders."

The loud squeals she could hear were coming from Bouncepaw, Tinypaw, and Rockpaw, who were chasing one another in a tight circle, their fur bristling with excitement. As Leafstar watched, their mother, Clovertail, padded up to them, her whiskers twitching anxiously. Leafstar couldn't hear what she said, but the apprentices skidded to a halt; Clovertail beckoned Tinypaw with a flick of her tail, and started to give her face a thorough wash. Leafstar purred with amusement as the young white she-cat wriggled under the swipes of her mother's rough tongue, while Clovertail's eyes shone with pride.

Pebbles pattering down beside her startled Leafstar. Looking up, she saw Patchfoot heading down the rocky trail with a squirrel clamped firmly in his jaws. Waspwhisker followed him, with his apprentice, Mintpaw, a paw step behind; they both carried mice. Leafstar gave a little nod of approval as the hunting patrol passed her. Prey was becoming more plentiful with the warmer weather, and the fresh-kill pile was swelling. She pictured Waspwhisker when he had first joined the Clan during the first snowfall of leaf-bare: a lost kittypet wailing with cold and hunger as he blundered along the gorge. Now the gray-and-white tom was one of the most skillful hunters in the Clan, with an apprentice of his own. He even had kits, with another former stray named Fallowfern.

SkyClan is growing.

As their father padded past, Waspwhisker's four kits bounced out of the nursery and scampered behind him, squeaking. Their mother, Fallowfern, emerged more slowly and edged her way down the trail after them; she still wasn't completely comfortable with the sheer cliff face and pointed rocks that surrounded SkyClan's camp.

"Be careful!" she called. "Don't fall!"

The kits had already reached the bottom of the gorge, getting under their father's paws, cuffing one another over the head and rolling over perilously near to the pool. Waspwhisker gently nudged the pale brown tom, Nettlekit, away from the edge.

But as soon as their father turned away to drop his prey on the fresh-kill pile, Nettlekit's sister Plumkit jumped on him. Nettlekit swiped at her, as if he was trying to copy a battle move he'd seen when the apprentices were training. Plumkit rolled over; Nettlekit staggered, lost his balance, and toppled into the river.

Fallowfern let out a wail. "Nettlekit!"

Stifling a gasp, Leafstar sprang to her paws, but she was too far away to do anything. Fallowfern leaped swiftly from boulder to boulder, but Waspwhisker was faster still, plunging into the pool after his kit. Leafstar lost sight of them for a few heartbeats. She watched the other Clan cats huddled at the water's edge—all except for Shrewtooth, who paced up and down the bank, his tail lashing in agitation. Leafstar purred with relief when she saw Waspwhisker hauling himself out of the river with Nettlekit clamped firmly in his jaws. The tiny tom's paws flailed until his father set him down on the rock. Then he shook himself, spattering every cat with shining drops of water. Fallowfern pounced on him and started to lick his pelt, but Nettlekit struggled away from her and hurled himself straight at Plumkit.

"I'll teach you to push me in the river!" he squealed.

"I did not push you! You fell in, so there!" Plumkit yowled back. She crouched down and leaped forward to meet her littermate in midair. The two kits tussled together in a knot of fur while their parents, looking frustrated, tried to separate them.

Leafstar glanced over her shoulder at the sound of paw steps approaching from farther down the gorge and saw Echosong with a bundle of herbs in her mouth. The young medicine cat's soft fur shone in the sunlight, reminding Leafstar that not long ago she had been a kittypet. But now she moved confidently over the stony ground, her pads hardened by her time in the gorge, and she had the lean, muscular strength of a Clan cat.

Echosong looked up at her Clan leader. "Greetings, Leafstar!" she called, her voice blurred by the herbs.

"Greetings!" Leafstar meowed back to her. "We'll start the warrior ceremony soon."

Echosong acknowledged her words with a wave of her tail, and vanished into her den near the bottom of the cliff to add the herbs to her store.

"Are you ready?"

Leafstar started as a voice spoke at her shoulder, and spun around to see her deputy, Sharpclaw, standing behind her. She hadn't noticed his silent approach. "Oh, it's you," she meowed. "You frightened my fur off, creeping up on me like that!"

The dark ginger tom narrowed his eyes in amusement. "Nothing frightens your fur off, Leafstar." With a glance at the sky, he added, "It's sunhigh. When are you going to start the ceremony?"

"I'm waiting for the others," Leafstar explained.

Sharpclaw's amusement vanished and he flicked his tail. "You should carry on without them," he meowed impatiently.

Leafstar twitched one ear in surprise, and saw a defensive look come into her deputy's eyes.

"We never know when they're going to turn up," he persisted. "And there are three young cats down there ready to burst with excitement."

Glancing at the Rockpile again, Leafstar saw that he was right. Bouncepaw and Rockpaw were circling each other as if they were about to start battle training, while Tinypaw bounced up and down on the spot, too anxious to sit still. Their shrill mews floated up to Leafstar.

"Very well." Leafstar dipped her head. "We'll start now."

With one more glance at the top of the gorge, she led the way down the trail to the Rockpile. As she and Sharpclaw approached, their Clanmates parted to let them through. Leafstar bunched her muscles and sprang to the top of the rocks, while Sharpclaw took his place at the base, not far from the fresh-kill pile. From the Rockpile, Leafstar looked down at her deputy's broad shoulders, and felt a stab of gratitude for his courage and loyalty.

He's a good deputy. Firestar advised me well.